RED SHIFT

DELIA STRANGE

Paperback ISBN: 978-1-7637236-7-2
Digital ISBN: 978-1-7637236-8-9

www.DeliaStrange.com

1231 Publishing
PO Box 77
Kallangur Q 4503
AUSTRALIA

CONTENTS

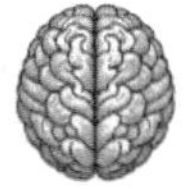

GIFT TO THE WORLD

Hors d'oeuvres on silver platters were carried around the room by white gloved hands. Dr Tina Merriman, dressed in a glittering emerald gown and holding a flute of champagne, looked down at the crowd below. Perhaps two hundred people were assembled on the street, punching fists into the air or holding signs with misspelt phrases. Dr Mark Abbot joined her side and glanced at the crowd before tipping his wine glass in her direction.

"This is the thanks we get for the gift we gave to the world."

"They're angry because they're frightened."

"And they're frightened because they're ignorant," Mark finished, his scorn apparent. Tina pulled her gaze from the window to look at him. A brilliant surgeon but like so many of his kind; arrogant. She believed the public's fears were founded. A corrupt medical system would never allow all those who needed a brain transplant to have it; for now, her success would be reserved only for the rich. Maybe one day the cost would lower enough for everybody to have access to a life-saving procedure.

"Come, we're supposed to give speeches and have photos taken," Mark encouraged, offering his arm. "It's good to be young, smart and beautiful."

Tina puffed laughter as Mark leant into his conceit. The waggling of his eyebrows had her giggling before she took his arm. They joined the group of four other doctors who were part of her team, each holding an etched rectangular trophy that was the Edison award. Flashbulbs blinded her and she smiled through it until it got too much. The white light was persistent, and she closed her eyes with a soft click.

"Do you know where you are?" an unfamiliar voice asked.

The strange question had Tina opening her eyes. Yet another soft click sounded. Instead of a room full of elegantly dressed innovators at the top of their fields, she saw two women in lab coats peering at her. The blonde one held a small torch for testing eye reflexes.

"What's going on? How did I get here?" Tina tried to shield her face, but her arm was too heavy. Had there been something in her alcohol? Had she been doped and kidnapped? Why had she been squirrelled away into a room full of computer equipment?

"It's okay, you're safe," the blonde said gently. She clicked the torch off and pocketed it. "Can you tell me who you are?"

"Dr Tina Merriman."

"Very good," the woman smiled, her tone reminding Tina of carers who work with the very young or the very old. "Do you know what year it is?"

"It's 2025. What happened? Did the protest get violent?" She imagined an attack where she might've been concussed. It wasn't unusual to get partial amnesia and feel confused. Seeing the way the two women looked at one another made her anxious. She didn't feel confusion so much as a lack of clarity. One of the women stepped away, closer to the computers. Tina took a breath to calm herself and heard a strange whirring. She needed answers and panicking wasn't the way to get them. "I would like to know what happened."

The blonde nodded.

"There was a bombing and you were on the cusp of the affected area."

A bombing! Tina gasped and heard the whirring sound again. Where was that coming from?

"You're suffering from some memory loss— not uncommon in these circumstances. Your memories should return soon. You might get them back scattered or all in one go. If you need help we're only a phone call away. I must say you've inspired me my whole life."

Her whole life? Tina stared at the woman who looked to be somewhere in her late twenties. Tina hadn't been recognised for her achievements until tonight. She recalled the way the two of them had looked at each other when she'd answered the question about the year.

"What year is it?"

"It's 2081."

The answer was so ridiculous that Tina burst into laughter. "In 2081 I'd be ninety years old!" she exclaimed through her mirth. She didn't feel like a ninety-year-old woman.

"Her math is on point," the other woman said. Tina's gaze flicked to watch her making peculiar gestures in the air. There was nothing she was manipulating as far as Tina could see.

"Yes, Dr Merriman. That's right." The blonde woman patted Tina's hand, but she couldn't feel it. She recognised the movement from the way the blonde's arm shifted forward but the lack of sensation was worrying. Tina looked downward and all coherent thought left her.

There was a mechanical body—a *robot* body—where her human one should have been. No clothes were necessary to cover up the white glossy shell that she inhabited. Was that why she couldn't lift her hand earlier? It was heavier than usual? She splayed her fingers and watched as the fingers on the robot hand spread out.

"What? Get me... this is ludicrous, how did?" And then it clicked. Tension left her body. "This is a dream. Of course." Tina laughed again, feeling hysteria bubbling within.

"The trauma could have caused a dissociative disorder," the gesturing woman said. The blonde frowned and shook her head, holding Tina's robot hand.

"Tina, please. You are not dreaming. I understand this is a shock, but you'll remember soon." The blonde leant forward, peering into Tina's eyes like she might be able to see something human in them. "Do you remember discovering how to transplant a human brain?"

"Of course, I do. I was just at the awards dinner, celebrating." Tina looked around the room. Every wall was covered in computer equipment. Machines she didn't recognise with readouts she didn't understand. They did look kind of... futuristic. "But that was about saving lives, not making robot abominations!"

"Tina, look at me. Tina, please look at me." The blonde gave a worried smile when Tina stared at her once more. "You are not an abomination. You have saved many, many lives. There were problems at the start, do you remember? The first ten years were riddled with rejections and suicides. A law passed in 2038 that no living creature should receive a brain transplant. Your husband saved your work when he invented a biochemical fluid that the brain could survive in, so transplants are now placed into artificial containers."

There was so much to unpack in that explanation that Tina could only stare at the woman for a long moment.

"My husband?" she asked finally.

"Yes, we've called him to let him know you're

alright. He's sent a car to pick you up."

"Who am I married to?" Tina asked, wondering if she would recognise the name.

"To Dr Mark Abbott."

"Mark? I married Mark?" Tina laughed. "This *must* be a dream. I'd never marry him!"

The blonde, still holding onto Tina's robot hand, spoke over her shoulder at the other woman. "What are her nominals?"

Her nominals? That didn't even make sense. Had language changed in fifty-six years? She supposed certain words did morph. Why was she even entertaining this? It was a dream. Dreams didn't follow logic. There was relief in that thought.

"Steady. Almost perfect, actually." The other woman stopped gesturing to shrug at the blonde. "The EMP didn't do any damage to her. Apart from the memory loss, she's fine."

"Can I go now?" Tina prompted, wanting to progress the dream to a different stage. She'd never had the opportunity to control a dream before and it was surprisingly difficult. She was wary of getting up and walking out in case the robot body didn't comply with her wishes.

"I don't feel comfortable with the idea of you wandering around the city with such a huge gap in your memory," the blonde said, standing straight. "Please wait here until your car arrives."

Tina, who'd worked with patients herself many times, knew that protesting would get her nowhere. Besides, she'd wake up and the dream would be over.

While waiting she discovered that taking a breath made something whirr inside of her. Robots didn't need to breathe so something else must've been happening. Maybe she was oiling herself. She laughed softly and caught the attention of the two women.

"Just had a funny thought."

"A memory?" the blonde prompted.

Tina shook her head and the two of them went back to whatever they were doing with the equipment. She heard a car rolling up outside, tyres on bitumen.

"Okay, your ride's here," the blonde said, moving towards her. She unplugged something out of Tina's shoulder—it was the first time she felt a physical sensation. The blonde spoke as she headed for the door. "A technician will drop by your place in the next couple of days to see how you're going. Take it easy in the meantime."

"It was an honour meeting you, Dr Merriman," the woman at the computers said.

Cautiously, Tina leant forward in the chair, getting ready to stand. There was a sensation of weightiness before she stood to her full height, perfectly balanced. She took a tentative step towards the door the blonde had opened for her and saw the city lights beyond.

She stepped down onto the street and looked back to discover the room she'd been in was actually a vehicle. It reminded her of an ambulance, painted white with blue and red lights on top, but the word TECHNICIANS was emblazoned along the side in red. The blonde remained in the doorway, watching her expectantly.

Tina turned back to look at the car in front of her. It still looked like a car, albeit rounder at the back and squatter at the front. She entered the opening and sat on the forward-facing seat. The car door slid shut and it quietly propelled forward even though she was the only one in the car.

Out the window she saw a city she still recognised, though there were a few extra buildings. Interspersed among the people were a lot of white robot bodies. She noticed a robot animal on a lead and stared at it, wondering what it meant. Were brain transplants now so accessible that people could get them for their pets? The idea was appalling; animals couldn't give consent.

A billboard on a low roof caught her attention and she stared at it, horrified. There was a picture of a robot body, very similar to her own, with encouraging words emblazoned beneath.

Got aches and pains? Buy the EB-4.2 model before your own body gives out!

"Aches and pains?" Tina whispered. Were people getting brain transplants because they felt the onset of aging? Was this dream a portent of how her discovery could be abused? Would people in the future really treat it like a cosmetic procedure or a ticket to eternal life? Would they keep upgrading themselves until their minds gave out? And what about those who would struggle with the transition? What kind of psychological impacts was society opening itself up to?

"This is not real. I'm dreaming," Tina insisted, but there was a harsh quality to this dream that she didn't recognise from others, which were soft and hazy and weird. She could feel her anxiety clawing up inside of her and sitting on her chest, making her feel like she couldn't breathe. But she didn't need to breathe, did she? She was a robot.

She didn't *feel* like a ninety-year-old woman, but since her brain was now encased in an artificial husk, there was no way to get the sensation of age other than through memory, and her memories were gone. What had the blonde technician said? There'd been a bombing. An EMP had gone off; an electro-magnetic pulse, something that didn't harm humans but shut down everything electronic.

She remembered looking down at the protestors from the function room. She remembered their anger, their fear. She'd called herself an abomination to the technician, who'd strongly disagreed. But those people, those *terrorists* who'd set off the bomb, they would agree with her. They would spout some religious passage to justify the murder. And it *was* murder, because even if they looked like robots, the minds inside belonged to people.

Tina conceded it would be difficult to see them that way, even if the robots were made to look as human as possible. She could imagine the kind of problems society would have with them. She wished she'd been aware enough to ask the technicians if robots had lost any human rights.

The city gave way to a highway which then turned into suburbs. The houses grew larger as the car changed streets. It pulled into a driveway of a house that looked like a pile of white blocks left behind by a giant child. There was a pretentious hologram of a fountain in the front yard. That had to be Mark's doing.

The door opened and a strangely familiar middle-aged man hurried out, followed by a woman Tina didn't recognise and two teenagers closely behind. As she stepped out of the car and was hugged by the man whose arms she could not feel, she deduced they were her children and grandchildren.

"Mum, holy muck, I'm glad you're alright," the hugger said. Tina wrapped careful arms around him and stared over his shoulder at the woman who looked like she'd been crying. Seemed like she had a good relationship with her daughter-in-law. The teens watched from their mother's side.

"Where's Mark?" Tina said, again feeling like this might be a dream after all.

"The house," her son said, stepping back and holding onto her arms. He was giving her an odd look. "Are you alright? The technicians said you had some memory loss?"

She gave the man a studious look. Her dreaming mind had done a good job of making him look like a perfect combination of Mark and herself. How delightful!

"I'm alright, I just need a nap."

"A nap?" her son repeated slowly.

"You know what I mean," Tina hazarded. "I've

momentarily lost the word."

"Downtime?" he provided.

"Yes. Downtime." Tina looked towards the front door, but Mark was nowhere to be seen. She'd thought he would come out here to greet her like her son and his family. It was strange that they were even here. She'd expected to see Mark and nobody else. "Do you live here with us?" she asked. "I have a few holes in my memory, but they are starting to come back," she lied.

"Oh, okay," her son said, sounding like it was very not okay. "Yes, you wanted us with you after your transition," he said, gesturing at her.

"Right," she said, now wondering if Mark had made the transition, too. It didn't explain why his white metal backside wasn't out here, though. "Let's go find your father."

"*Find* him?" her son repeated.

Tina sighed and caused a whirr to go off inside her chest. She marched into the house with her insta-family trailing behind her.

"Mark?" she called out from the foyer. The house was exceptionally beautiful on the inside.

"Yes, Tina?" Mark's voice replied. Tina looked up and around but saw nothing.

"Where are you?"

"All around you, my love," he said.

"What? Are you plugged into the house?" she guessed, getting the hang of this dream.

Tina felt a pull to one side and turned, seeing that her son had tugged on her arm. "Mum, don't you remember? He *is* the house. We live in him."

SALT AND SILENCE

12 June, 1810

Commander Hugh Markham stood on the quarterdeck, his vantage point allowing him to see most of the deck of the *HMS Resolute*. The early morning mist hung like a shroud over the waves. Even in the eerie stillness, there were sounds of life all around him. Men called out to one another as they performed their duties, the ship creaked as it swayed, and the gulls cried their dissent overhead.

"Sir!" Lieutenant Avery, stationed at the bow, sought Markham's attention. "Vessel spotted, bearing northeast!"

Markham retrieved his telescope from his coat and moved to Avery's side. He raised the instrument to his eye, spying a small vessel in the distance, its sails slack.

"Unanchored," Avery muttered beside him. "Odd. No sign of a crew, Commander."

Markham focused the lens, studying the sloop. The sails were intact, the hull sound, yet there was no movement aboard—no figures bustling about, no one adjusting rigging or watching the seas.

Markham pressed his lips together as he lowered the telescope, then glanced at Avery. "A derelict that's seaworthy? That shouldn't be."

He snapped the instrument shut and returned it to his coat. "Lieutenant, bring us alongside with caution. Prepare to board. I'll not risk losing men to foolish haste."

"Aye, sir."

The *Resolute* closed the distance to the drifting sloop. Ropes were made ready, grapples coiled, and the boarding party armed.

As they got nearer, Markham saw the sloop's

name was *Silence*. He puffed a humourless laugh, made uneasy by the apt naming.

Markham stepped onto the deck of the sloop behind his marines, his boots echoing hollowly on the planks. The air was thick with the tang of salt and the faint musk of damp wood. His hand rested on the hilt of his sword, the only outward display of his unease. His face impassive as gut roiled and heart hammered.

The marines spread out, moving cautiously across the deck. Avery bent to examine a coil of rope that lay undisturbed near the foremast. "Everything's in place," the lieutenant observed. "As if they'd left for just a moment."

Markham's gaze swept the deck. Below the hatch leading to the cargo hold, he spotted crates stacked in an orderly fashion. It was almost too normal.

"Sir!" came a call from the starboard side. A marine stood by an open crate, holding up a bottle. "Brandy, sir. And Genever by the smell of it. Smugglers' stock."

The commander strode over, taking the bottle and turning it in his hands. The label bore a Dutch mark. "So, they were smugglers. But where are they now?"

Avery shook his head. "No signs of struggle. No blood. No lifeboat missing either."

Markham's fingers tightened around the bottle. This wasn't the first smuggling vessel he'd intercepted, but it was the first he'd found utterly abandoned. He cast his gaze toward the horizon, half expecting to see another ship or a storm cloud—some sign of what had occurred—but the sea was empty and calm.

"This ship is sound," he said finally. "She could've sailed home on her own. And yet here she drifts." He returned the bottle to the marine. "Secure the cargo. No tampering. I want the hold catalogued."

Back aboard his own ship, Markham gave his final order: "Gather every document aboard. Logs, letters, even scraps of paper. Sort them by date and deliver them to my quarters. I want to know everything about this vessel."

The officers and marines nodded, moving with grim efficiency. Markham turned away with a frown. A derelict was one thing. A seaworthy sloop, abandoned without cause, was another altogether.

He paused at the door to his cabin, glancing over his shoulder toward the silent sloop one last time. Whatever answers lay within those papers, he resolved to uncover them.

That evening, as the sun dipped below the horizon and cast the cabin in a deep amber glow,

Lieutenant Avery knocked firmly at the Commander's door. At Markham's acknowledgment, Avery stepped inside, a neat bundle of papers and books tied together with twine, tucked under an arm.

"Sir," Avery began, placing the bundle on the desk. "The sloop has been lashed securely to the Resolute. During a more thorough search of her hold, we uncovered another part of the cargo—a crate of Icelandic spar. Our surgeon identified it as valuable, though I'm no expert on the matter." His tone was matter-of-fact, but his brow furrowed, betraying unease.

Markham looked up from his chair, eyes narrowing. "Spar, you say. Curious. Anything else?"

Avery shook his head. "No, sir. Aside from the cargo and a distinct lack of answers, the sloop seems in fine order."

Markham nodded. "Very well, Lieutenant. My thanks. Ensure the men remain vigilant tonight. I'll want another sweep come morning."

"Yes, sir." Avery straightened, saluted, and exited.

Markham exhaled, listening to the faint creak of the ship's timbers. His hand moved to the bundle, pausing before pulling the twine free. The papers spilled slightly, revealing a mix of journals, notes, and letters, some smudged with seawater, others preserved with care.

He began with the logbook, running his eye along the muster roll.

Elias Sutton, Captain/Navigator
Thomas Garrow, First Mate/Bosun
Alfred Colson, Helmsman
Cedric Bell, Surgeon
Fergus 'Flint' Macrae, Gunnar
Edward 'Ned' Morris, Powder Monkey
Robert Henshaw, Cook
Geoffrey Maddox, Senior Deckhand
Sameul Dawkins, Deckhand/Rigger
James Colson, Rigger/Cabin Boy

Ten men, a small crew but still capable enough to manage a sloop. Markham looked through the logbook but didn't have the stomach for the inaccuracies. Smugglers tended not to log their ill-doings.

He set the logbook aside and picked up the first letter, its handwriting precise but hurried. The faintest scent of brine lingered on the paper as he unfolded it.

8th June, 1810
My Dearest Margaret,

You'll forgive me, I hope, for not writing when I'm away. Our trips are usually short, and there's little to say once I've returned. This time, things are different. The captain's taken us farther afield—to the Faroes, of all places—for a special cargo that's worth more than the rest of the ship put together. It's extended the journey considerably, which means I have time to write to you.

I must tell you what happened last night, though I fear my words won't capture the mood. Around the second watch, Sammy spotted something adrift in the water—a lifeboat, of all things. It looked to be floating aimlessly. When we came up alongside it, we found a boy inside. The poor lad looked scared, but didn't make a sound.

Maddox was the one who climbed down the rope ladder to fetch him. You know Maddox—strong as an ox, steady as a rock. It had to be him. Jimmy or Sammy climb the rigging like monkeys, but carrying the boy up would've been too much for either of them. Maddox hoisted the boy up as easy as lifting a sack of flour, though I could see the lad was light enough to blow away in a stiff wind.

When they got him on deck, you'd have thought we'd caught a mermaid for the way the others crowded around to see. The boy didn't speak, just

Markham leant back in his chair, Tom Garrow's letter still in hand. Four days. The letter was dated only four days ago. What in God's name could have happened in so short a time to leave the sloop adrift and abandoned? He turned the letter over absently, as though the reverse might offer some revelation. Finding none, he set it aside and reached for the next document.

The handwriting struck him first, neat and precise. A professional's hand, no doubt the surgeon's. Markham let the irritation bristle through him when he saw the date: 7 June, one day prior to Garrow's account. The inconsistency gnawed at him until he considered Avery's meticulous nature. No doubt the lieutenant had been puzzled by the report and sought to find some kind of explanation, so he'd muddled the order for context. Begrudgingly, Markham approved. He adjusted his posture and began to read.

Medical Report: 7 June, 1810
Surgeon's Quarters, aboard the *Silence*
Subject: Male child, approximate age 8 years
Condition on Arrival:
- General Appearance: Severely underweight, visibly hollow-eyed, pale. No visible injuries or marks upon initial inspection.
- Temperature: Skin unusually cold to the touch, consistent across extremities and torso. Despite this, pulse and respiration remain steady and within normal parameters.
- Behaviour: Silent, unresponsive to verbal inquiry. Alert but withdrawn, with an evident reluctance to engage.
Actions Taken:
Provision of Sustenance:
- Offered water and a small meal (salt pork and hardtack). Subject consumed both rapidly, suggestive of prolonged deprivation.

- Observed no signs of difficulty swallowing or digestive distress following consumption.

Accommodation:

- Provided subject with a woollen blanket for warmth.

- Allocated the spare cot in the surgeon's quarters, given his fragile state.

Prognosis and Recommendations:

- Immediate need for rest and ongoing nourishment.

- Subject's silence and cold skin temperature warrant further observation. No evidence yet of injury or illness.

Additional Notes:

The boy's silence is troubling but may be due to trauma or exhaustion. Further observation is required.

Signed: Dr. Cedric Bell, Surgeon

Markham exhaled as he considered the report. There was a clinical detachment to the surgeon's words, but between the lines lay a grim picture: a boy adrift at sea, half-starved, mute, yet somehow unscathed. The detail about his skin—cold, but with normal vitals—grated at his sense of reason.

He tapped the report lightly against the desk and moved to the next document. The answers he sought had to be here, somewhere.

Markham sifted through the stack of papers with growing unease. Scribbled orders and crude sketches offered little insight, likely notes between deckhands. He brushed them aside, pausing only when he came upon a neatly written medicinal recipe.

It was simple, likely penned by the doctor—a mixture for a basic tonic, judging by the ingredients listed. What use was a recipe to understanding the fate of the sloop? He flipped it over, expecting nothing, but discovered a hastily written note on the underside, the handwriting rough and angular, clearly belonging to another hand.

Have to tell someone about the lad. There's a rongness to him. This morn, I went to the galley to prep first meal, and there he was. Rapt in a blanket, quiet as a mouse. Or a rat. He din't touch nothing but seeing him there turnt my stomach.

I told him plain he ought to be back with the doc. He din't speak, just looked at me. It itched my skin. Din't want to touch him, but din't want to leave him there. Walked him back to the doc and said nothing. Wish to God we din't pull him aboard.

Markham reread the note twice, each word

pulling at him. The cook's misgivings mirrored the peculiarities in the surgeon's report—a mute boy, out of place, and unsettling in ways no physical description could justify.

He turned the recipe over again. Smugglers weren't men prone to dramatics, but the tone of the note suggested discomfort beyond reason. A seasoned sailor, unnerved by the mere presence of a child?

Each piece of the puzzle only deepened the mystery, and he was certain now that something had happened on that sloop that was more than smuggling or desertion.

He arrived at the journal, and he opened it, flipping past pages until he arrived at a relevant date, reading the first entry since the boy's rescue.

8 June, 1810

The sun sinks, bleeding its last light into the western sky, and the men have gathered below deck for their second meal. There is a heaviness in the air tonight, though the wind is calm and the seas obliging. Since last night, when we brought the boy aboard, a peculiar mood has taken hold of the crew. Maddox, who prides himself on being as unshakable as stone, glanced twice over his shoulder during his watch this morning, and

Henshaw, usually as jovial as the rum he cooks with, muttered something beneath his breath and checks the corners. He doesn't visit Bell for his education anymore. Perhaps a criticism went over too harshly? Even as I write this, I think not.

Tom holds the helm now in place of Alfred Colson. Tom is a steady hand amid the unease. I will dine with him later, as is our habit, once the men have finished their meal and a small number return to their duties. He is a reliable man, and his company offers a balm to my thoughts when they grow too clouded.

It was while I wrote this, just now, that I heard it—soft at first, but unmistakable. The rhythmic clop of hooves on deck, as though a horse had found its way aboard. I laid my pen aside, frowning at the absurdity of it. A horse? Here, on a sloop, miles from the nearest stable? Yet the sound came again, faint but deliberate, and I could no longer ignore it.

I left my cabin, the journal open on my desk, and climbed to the deck. The evening air was cool and sharp with salt, and the sea stretched indifferently around us. I stood still, straining to hear it again—the clopping—but the deck lay silent.

Puzzled, I walked the length of the ship, half-

expecting to find a rope or barrel come loose, tapping against the wood in some trick of the wind. But there was nothing out of place. The ship was as tidy and orderly as it had been all day.

Tom saw me and called out, "All's well, Captain?" His voice was steady, but his brow furrowed as he watched me. I offered a brief nod and returned below.

I had nearly reached my quarters when I met Flint standing by the galley stairs with his arms crossed.

"Evening, Captain," he said, his tone lighter than his expression. "Did you hear it too?"

"Hear what?" I asked.

He shifted, glancing toward the galley. "Singing. Went on for a bit, then stopped. None of the pigs down there came for a look with me, they're still at it with their dinner."

His words gave me pause. Singing? I shook my head and told him to carry on, then returned to my quarters.

Now, as I sit here with my pen, I cannot make sense of it. What I heard was the sound of hooves—I am certain of it. As a fair horseman, I know the cadence well, the way the hooves strike with a particular rhythm. But there are no horses aboard, nor should there be.

I shall end this entry here. Perhaps it was

nothing but a trick of the wind.

Markham paused and leant back in his chair, staring at the dim lamplight flickering against the bulkhead. A trick of the wind? It was the simplest explanation, and one he would likely make himself, but his gut twisted against it. Hooves on the deck, hollow and deliberate—no wind could mimic that sound. Yet, what else could it have been?

He let his gaze drift back to the book open on his desk. His eyes snagged on words scrawled in the next entry: "...a horse..."

His breath caught and he checked the date.

9 June, 1810

The promise of clarity pulled at him like a thread unravelling a well-worn fabric. Slowly, deliberately, he read on.

I scarcely know how to begin. How can I set to paper the events of this morning, so impossible they seem even now? Three of my men are lost to the sea, taken before our very eyes in a manner I can scarcely credit. The air in my cabin feels heavier, the walls closer, and my pen trembles as I write this. Yet I must. If I do not, I fear the truth of it will slip away entirely, as though the events themselves were no more than a cruel dream.

I was on my way to visit Bell and the boy. The morning sky was flat white but calm, and I thought to check on the lad. I was interrupted by shouts from above—cheers and jeers mingled with the unmistakable sound of commotion.

I was certain that Maddox, who had the deck, would bring order swiftly enough. Tom slept below after taking shift at the helm last night, so Maddox was in charge. But there was no bark of command.

Curious, I rose and made for the deck. What I saw when I emerged will stay with me until my dying day.

Five of the crew stood gathered near the bow, circling something. Their shouts were rowdy, filled with astonishment and delight. As I approached, the group parted slightly, and there, standing docile and unbothered by the chaos, was a horse.

A grey horse, smaller and sturdier than those I've ridden before, like a workhorse built for pulling heavy loads. Its long mane fell thickly over its eyes, veiling them entirely, and it stood as though carved from stone. It bore no saddle, no bridle.

The sight struck me dumb. A horse? Impossible. My head swam with questions, but there was no time for answers. Samuel Dawkins was already clambering onto its back, grinning like a fool and shouting for young James Colson to join him. "Come on, Jimmy!" he whooped. "Don't be a coward now!"

Jimmy, ever eager to prove himself, scrambled up behind Dawkins.

In one swift, fluid motion, the horse sprang to life, slamming into Alfred Colson, who'd been near the beast's head. The man fell with a cry, clutching his shoulder as the horse galloped across the deck, towards me. Through the disturbance, I noticed its hooves were facing backward. It turned, then leapt clean over the rail and into the sea.

Jimmy and Dawkins screamed, their voices carrying over the water as the horse plunged beneath the waves. I will never forget their cries: "We can't get off! We're stuck! We're stuck!"

Stuck. As though glued to the beast.

For a moment, the deck was silent, the crew paralysed by what we had witnessed. I was the first to break the spell, shouting for the helm to be steadied and the ship turned around. "Search the water!" I bellowed. "We'll find them—God help us, we'll find them!"

The crew sprang to action. Men scrambled to adjust our course, their movements quick but orderly. Maddox, to his credit, held firm, directing the chaos with the steady voice I had expected earlier. But it was Alfred who gave us the greatest *trouble.*

He had risen and was halfway over the rail before Maddox yelled at him. He turned with a haunted look that I will see in my nightmares. "I need to fetch my boy!" Alfred roared.

And then he was gone.

We searched the water for what felt like hours, every pair of eyes scanning the waves for any sign of the Alfred or the young men. But there was nothing. No horse, no figures splashing on the surface, no floating bodies. The sea had swallowed them whole.

I write this now with the taste of failure bitter in my mouth. I have lost three of my crew, and I cannot even say how or why.

I must end here. My thoughts are clouded, and the men will need me soon.

Markham, who usually had no compassion for smugglers, felt empathy for Sutton. Losing crew was hard on any captain, and the circumstances of Sutton's loss were unusual to say the least. He would've dismissed the journal entries as the ravings of a lunatic, except Sutton's writing seemed sound, and the other letters backed him. His eyes landed on the next letter in line, placed in between the journal pages. A quick look at the signature confirmed it was written by Bell, the surgeon.

9 June, 1810

To Whomever It May Concern,

I have little need for journalling, but given the peculiar nature of recent events, I am compelled to make a record. The boy, whom we took aboard days ago, has proven a challenge—not in his physical condition, but in his behaviour.

He disappears now and then, wandering the ship. Each time, he is brought back by a member of the crew. My questions go unanswered, and though I've attempted to coax words from him with food, warmth, and patience, I am met with nothing but those hollow eyes and that oppressive quiet.

One thing is clear: the boy is deeply afraid of fire. He recoils from lanterns and is quick to retreat from them, even when I've tried to light the corner of my quarters. I suspect he may have been aboard a burning vessel before we found him— such a trauma would explain his silence and aversion.

Now, to the matter of his disappearance. Since this morning's tragedy, the boy has gone missing, and despite the crew's search, he has not been found. I will grant that the men's hearts are not entirely in the task—three lives lost in one day will!

Markham put the letter down and drummed his fingers lightly on the desk. His eyes lingered on the journal in front of him.

A letter poked out slightly from within the book, its corner creased and smudged.

Something about it pulled at him—a faint whisper of urgency, as though the letter itself carried the weight of an unanswered question.

He had no doubt he would have most answers by the end. The letters and entries were candid, despite their strangeness. The captain's words deserved their due first, and Markham would not indulge curiosity over order.

10 June, 1810

To Whoever may read this, if there is anyone left to do so,

My men have gone mad. God help me, perhaps I have too, for what I believe I have seen defies all reason. I write this now, not for posterity, but as an anchor to my sanity, though even as I set pen to paper, I feel it slipping.

The boy is gone. Disappeared. Bell took it upon himself to search for him after the morning's tragedy, but so far, he has found nothing. The men say little openly, but I hear the whispers, see the way they glance over their shoulders. I know what they think. To them, the boy is a curse, a harbinger of our ruin.

I saw it boil over not an hour ago. Henshaw stood by the galley, knife in hand, arguing with Tom. His voice was sharp, bitter, his words laced with a fear he would not admit. "We never should've pulled him aboard!" he spat. "It's him! The boy's done this to us!"

Tom, to his credit, stood calm and steady, though I saw the tension in his stance, the coiled strength in his frame. He was waiting, watching, preparing for the worst, but Henshaw did not strike. Instead, he turned abruptly, muttering as he stalked away.

Tom met my gaze then, his expression grim, and came to me. "Captain," he said quietly, his voice low so the others would not hear, "we need to find that boy, and fast. If we don't, the men will do it for us. And they'll throw him overboard."

For a moment, I thought to myself that perhaps they should. God forgive me, the thought came unbidden, but reason prevailed. "You're right," I said. "We'll search together."

The two of us spent what felt like hours combing the ship, looking in every corner, every shadowed space. The boy was nowhere to be found, but the tension among the crew only grew.

Then I heard it—a shout, sharp and unmistakable. Flint's voice. Fergus Macrae, my gunner, his thick Scottish brogue carrying over the creak of the ship's timbers. I recognised it instantly.

Tom and I ran to the deck, Maddox already there, his hands raised as he pleaded with Flint to come down. Flint stood on the railing, one hand clutching a rope for balance, the other gesturing wildly at nothing. His face was pale, his eyes wide, almost feverish.

"Flint!" I called, stepping forward. "What in God's name are you doing?"

He turned to me, his expression a strange mixture of terror and exhilaration. "Can ye no hear it, Captain?" he said, his voice trembling. "The song! Can ye no hear the song?"

I heard nothing but the wind and the groaning of the ship. "There's no song, Flint," I said. "Don't listen to it. It's in your head, a trick of the sea. You know the tales—Sirens, luring men to their deaths."

Flint laughed then, a sharp, humourless sound. "Sirens?" he said. "It's no Siren. It's that fucking horse. The Nykur. And there's no escaping it, Captain. We're surrounded by water. All this water!"

I froze. "The horse?" I asked, and took a step closer. "What is the Nykur?"

Flint didn't answer right away. He swayed slightly, as if to music I could not hear, his grip on the rope slackening. Then he looked at me again, his expression strangely calm. "I'm not afraid to die, Captain," he said. "It's the pain of the dying I'm not keen on. There'll be no pain, if I'm willing."

And before I could reply, he let go.

He fell into the water with a splash, his body disappearing beneath the waves.

We searched, of course. Maddox, Tom, and I scoured the sea for any sign of him. But there was nothing. The water swallowed him whole, as it did the others.

I write this now, my hands trembling, my heart heavy with fear and grief. What is happening to us? I no longer know what to believe.

The ship is crippled now, at the mercy of any who might come upon us. All our riggers are gone—Maddox and young Ned have taken their place, but it is a poor substitute for the men we have lost. Maddox is capable enough; he has subbed for the riggers on occasion, and his strength and steady nerves serve him well. But Ned... the boy is still reeling from Flint's death. He does his best, but his hands shake when he climbs, and I've seen him freeze halfway up the rigging more than once. He's fearful of heights, and his over-caution is likely to lead to an accident. I've half a mind to pull him down and forbid him from going up again, but what choice do I have?

There is no gunner now. With Flint gone, the weapons are left untended, though I doubt we'd muster the strength to use them even if we were attacked.

Tom has taken up the helm full-time, the bosun now our helmsman. Between him and I, we manage to keep the ship on course, but I can hardly call it sailing. The finer points of navigation and the precision of a steady wheel are lost when one's hands are always tied with other duties. I am no longer the captain and navigator but also the second helmsman and sometime bosun, and I feel the weight of it every moment.

The cook, Henshaw, has become a deckhand, much to his frustration. His years in the navy have given him the strength for the work, but he is no rigger, and his movements on deck lack the surety of the others. I see the resentment in his eyes—he feels his hands are wasted on rope and sail—but he has no room to argue.

Only Bell, our surgeon, has escaped the worst of the additional burdens. His hands are needed too desperately for their precision to risk him on deck. But even his duties, light as they are, go neglected. He spends his days searching for the boy, often disappearing for hours at a time as he crawls over every corner of the ship. He mutters constantly about finding him, as though the child holds some answer to the chaos that has engulfed us. I have tried talking to him, to draw his attention back to his work, but his obsession has taken root.

As I write this, the ship feels heavier than its

timber and cargo alone can explain. The air itself is laden with a sense of doom, and I find myself thinking, over and over, of the decision that brought us here.

The lure of so much money—enough to keep this crew fed and paid for years—drew me north to the Faroes. I told myself it was worth the risk, that the profits from the spar would justify the journey, that I owed it to my men to seize such an opportunity. But now? Now I see it for what it was. Greed, plain and simple.

I wish to God I had never gone. The promise of wealth has damned us all.

God forgive me.

Markham turned the page and read the next entry for that day, caught in a place of dismay and suspended belief.

10 June, 1810

It is night again. Tom is on the helm. There are fewer of us now—two more gone.

Ned is dead. The boy was too afraid of heights to be in the rigging, and I should never have let him up there. We're stretched too thin, every man doing work he wasn't meant for. Ned tangled himself in the ropes somehow and fell, hanging by his neck. Maddox got to him quickly, but there was no saving him.

Bell has vanished. No one knows when or how. The man was obsessed with finding the boy. He didn't show up for second meal. I ordered a search, half-hearted as it was. The men are spent, their nerves frayed, and he didn't answer any of the calls.

He's not aboard. He's gone. His obsession with the boy made him vulnerable.

But is the boy even a part of it? Perhaps he was set free from his own craft, trying to escape the curse that afflicted us. When we rescued him, did we invite something else onto the sloop? Is that what Bell wanted to ask him?

Tom came to my cabin to tell me what I already know. We're done. The ship is crippled. We have no riggers, no gunner, no surgeon. Even the cook is stretched thin, hauling sails and tying lines when he should be feeding us.

Tom suggested we toss the contraband and wait for the navy to find us. They might save us if we're flying a signal. I didn't answer him right away. I knew he was right. But there's no saving this crew. Not from this. Not from whatever we've brought aboard. Why would I damn another, as I have been damned? I don't dare.

I told him we'd discuss it at first light. God help us. God help me. I was the one who brought us here. It was all me. And now my men are dead, and those still alive will curse my name until they're gone, too.

I wish it ends soon. For all of us.

Markham leant back in his chair, pressing a hand to his forehead. The captain's final journal entry was a lot to consider. Sutton's words were filled with despair and guilt that resonated uncomfortably with the emptiness of the derelict sloop outside.

The Commander took a steadying breath and turned an empty page to get to the final letter. Unfolding the letter carefully, he recognised Tom's handwriting. A final message to his wife.

11th June, 1810
My Dearest Margaret,

I long to be with you again. I'm so sorry, love, for not coming home to you as I promised. I would give anything at all to walk through our door, kiss you, and hold our girls. But it's looking less and less likely. I don't know how much longer we have.

I need to tell you about last night. The boy I wrote about earlier, the one we saved from the lifeboat... we saw him again.

It started with footsteps, light as a child's, pattering across the deck. Then a thump, like something heavy hitting the boards. I ran up, not expecting to see... Margaret, it's terrible.

Sutton was in front of me, and the moment he got on deck he pulled out his pistol. I haven't told you, but he carries it everywhere now. He took it in his hand, and aimed squarely at something I couldn't see. When I joined his side, I saw he'd aimed it at Henshaw.

Henshaw—our cook, the man who's always singing and laughing—had the boy in one thick arm, pinned tight against his chest. The boy just hung there, his dirty, skinny legs dangling. Henshaw's other hand bore a knife. He sat upon the railing, readying to throw the child overboard.

Sutton shouted at him to stop, to think, to put the boy down. But Henshaw wouldn't listen. His face was pale, twisted with fear and desperation. I could see it in his eyes—he didn't want to do it. He's no child killer. But he didn't think the boy was human, and I don't know that I blame him.

"It was a horse that took them, not a boy!" Sutton cried out. I could hear the crack of desperation in his voice.

"The boy is the horse! He changes shape!" Henshaw argued, waggling the knife.

"That makes no sense, Bobby. Why would he change back to a boy? Why not something else— anything else?"

I know why he said these things, because they

were sensible, but Margaret, when a supernatural fear takes hold of a man, there's no logic that can come near it.

I could see Henshaw wrestling with himself, trying to muster the courage to strike.

"It's what Flint said, before he leapt. It's the Nykur."

The boy suddenly wriggled and fought, like he knew somehow that his life was at risk. His lips pulled back from his teeth and his feet clobbered against the side. Henshaw struggled and raised the knife to the boy's throat.

And then Sutton fired.

The shot rang out, it was so loud, Margaret, because I stood beside him. But I saw Henshaw jerk, his body stiffening as the bullet hit him. He toppled backward, and though I thought his arms would slacken and the boy would drop, instead he flipped over the side, taking the boy with him. They were gone in an instant, swallowed by the night sea.

Maddox, who was behind me, said, "Maybe it's over now." But I don't think it is. This morning, while I was at the helm, I saw something that made my heart cry out, knowing that we were lost after all.

On the deck below the railing where Henshaw fell, there were small, wet handprints.

I haven't told Sutton. He's stretched too thin, burdened with having shot one of his own men—someone he truly liked. He doesn't need to know about the handprints, not yet. And Maddox... Maddox is already out. He's into the rum now, drunk more often than not. I can't count on him for much anymore.

Margaret, I love you. Please tell the girls I love them too. Hold them close for me, tighter than ever. Pray for me, if you still can. Pray that I find a way to come home to you, even if I can't imagine how it will happen now.

Yours, always,

Tom

A shiver travelled throughout Markham's body, leaving behind an eerie sensation upon his flesh. He didn't know how long he sat with Tom's letter in his hands, but he jumped when a dull thump sounded against his door. The knock was followed almost immediately by the door opening, and Lieutenant Avery stepped inside without waiting to be summoned.

Markham's brow darkened as he stood. "Lieutenant, have you lost all sense of protocol?"

"I apologise, sir, but it's important," Avery said, his voice tight. He stepped forward, his hat clutched in his hands. "We found a survivor in one of the crates. We've pulled him out and brought him aboard."

Markham's eyes widened, and his pulse quickened. "A survivor? Well, then, who is it? Is it Sutton? No, it's Bell. It must be Bell."

Avery blinked, his confusion evident. "I can't say, sir. I'm not familiar with those names."

"Then describe him! Is he injured? Speak plainly, Lieutenant."

Avery hesitated, his expression troubled. "He hasn't said a word. He's... he's just a boy, Commander."

THE BUTCHER

News just in; the serial killer known as 'The Butcher' has been captured today in a massive search co-ordinated by local and state police. An anonymous tip led the authorities to where 'The Butcher' was hiding in a bushland shack. Sources say there is evidence of earlier, unknown kills, mounted on the walls like trophies.

When I stepped into the spartan room, my eyes

locked with those of the woman sitting at the table. A chain linked the cuffs on her wrists together, threaded through a thick metal ring welded onto the tabletop. She didn't look like a butcher. Her emaciated frame and haunted eyes gave her the appearance of a victim, not a perpetrator. Dirt hid her true colouring, but she did not smell like someone gone feral.

It was my responsibility to represent her, to give her a fair trial. It was a case that should not have gone to a novice lawyer such as myself, so I suspect the state wished for it to be over quickly. With barely three months on the job and a high-profile case in my lap, my name would forever be associated with hers. I trusted myself to be unbiased, however, so I didn't refuse the challenge like many of my associates.

"Good afternoon," I greeted cordially, eyeing the length of chain at her disposal. She could not reach me on the other side of the table and so I sat, setting my briefcase on my lap and pulling out the document of her arrest and a recording device. The guards had confiscated my pens.

She didn't reply, instead watching my every movement. The snap of the latches on my briefcase as they opened caused her to blink rapidly, and when they closed, she grunted her discontent.

"Do you... speak English?" I asked, my question faltering as I realised how useless any answer other than the affirmative would be. She surprised me by nodding once, perfunctorily. After checking the device was recording and setting my briefcase on the floor at my feet, I began.

"You've been identified as Lydia May Hartley. Is this correct?" She nodded again. "I'm sorry, but you'll have to speak up for the recording." I gestured at the device on the table.

"You're the first person to apologise to me," she said, her voice fractured with disuse. She cleared her throat and continued. "Yes, I am Lydia May Hartley."

I explained who I was and why I was there. Every time I prompted for whether she understood her rights or the proceedings as I explained them, she answered with a simple 'yes'. She was remarkably placid for a woman who'd allegedly taken a dozen lives.

"Did you kill them?" I asked.

"Yes."

The answer gave me pause even though I'd expected it. I'd been informed she'd not resisted arrest when the police arrived at her hideout. She'd opened the door upon their arrival and followed their every instruction.

"Why?"

"Because I was hungry and cold."

My stomach flipped in a way that left me sweating. I gripped the table and willed the nausea to pass. My throat tensed and I swallowed the saliva that flooded into my mouth. Once I had some semblance of control, I looked up to find a curious expression set upon her face.

I didn't want to clarify, but it was my job. I began to envy my peers who'd refused this case. I thought I'd had the stomach for gruesome details, but this was something else entirely.

"You ate them?" A numbness settled into my body even though my mind raced.

"Yes."

I imagined her crouched and tearing into raw, bloody flesh, but cast those images away. She sat before me like a reasonable human being, even as she admitted the evil of her actions. Like they weren't evil at all. Could she be criminally insane? Would this be my option for her?

I looked at the report before me, a copy of her arrest documentation. I flipped the page and read what the police had found at her shelter.

"Your hideout had a firepit near a vegetable garden—"

"It was my home, not a hideout."

Her interruption distracted me from my

course of questioning. "You lived in a shack in a forest?"

"It's a cabin, and yes."

"By yourself?"

"Yes."

"What was your means of transport?" I asked, anticipating that she wouldn't isolate herself from the rest of civilisation. She had to have a way of going into the closest town for supplies, but the report didn't mention any vehicles nearby.

"I didn't have any."

"How did you bring the bodies back to the shelter?"

"I carried them."

I re-assessed her. Of course she could be lying, but on the assumption of truth I saw some details about her that I had missed upon first entering the room. She was thin, but she wasn't frail. Her arms were sinewy with muscle.

"You see it now, don't you?" she asked, and I lifted my gaze to meet hers. "You see me the same way they do." The chain clinked as she gestured to the door towards where a police officer stood. "I saw the way your face changed. I'm finally a killer to you."

"You confessed to me, you can hardly take it back," I sputtered. Her outburst had not been of driven emotion. She'd spoken calmly, but her words were accusatory.

"I'm not taking it back. I did nothing wrong."

I was astonished. "You're not serious?" Even as I asked this, I knew she was. She had the look of conviction about her. While not a professional psychiatrist, I highly doubted she was fooling me. It had been in every one of her actions until this point; the way she'd answered her door, not resisted arrest, calmly spoke about her crimes, and added the insanity of how she'd eaten her victims. The trophies on her walls implied she'd skinned them as well.

"It's human to do what I did. Not that long ago we were eating meat and wearing fur and leather."

"It's forbidden to eat meat! It's illegal to extort animals!" I spoke as loudly as I dared, as though my volume could change her mind.

"I wasn't going to let myself starve to death or freeze over the winter," she said, as if slaughtering animals, skinning their fur and eating their flesh was a normal thing to do.

A LACK OF VISION

The wipers couldn't keep up with the deluge. The sound of rain upon her car reminded Jen of the applause from a home game, the way it drowned out all other noise. She squinted through the glass at the blurry shapes beyond, unable to see the painted lines on the road. She changed into the overtaking lane, anticipating the turn she would eventually have to make to get home. At least she could just make out the median strip on her side of the car.

Ash thumbed through Tik Tok videos beside her; every so often Jen's peripheral vision caught movement on the glowing screen in her sister's hand.

"Find something good?" Jen asked, elevating her voice so she could be heard.

"You should be watching the road," Ash lectured, not lifting her eyes from her phone.

"It's not like I can see anything," Jen mumbled her complaint, unwilling to get into an argument. As soon as the words were out of her mouth, she *did* see something; a shadow racing across the road, directly in front of her.

"What the—?" she cried out, stamping on the brake. The phone flew out of Ashley's hands and clattered along the dash. There was a muffled thud and then the front wheels bounced like they'd hit a speed bump.

For a long moment there was nothing but the sound of rain before Ash cried out, "What was that?"

"I don't know," Jen replied, staring at the rain-blurred glass before her. Her hands gripped the steering wheel so tightly that her knuckles shone white. *I don't want to know.*

Faintly, she could hear a man talking. Confusion and unreality washed over her. The man was laughing about something—she couldn't make out words but there was definitely a tone of amusement.

Understanding dawned when her gaze shifted and landed on Ashley's phone on the dash. It was still playing a video. She reached for it and pressed the button that put it to sleep.

Jen heard the distinct click of a seatbelt latch and the whirr of it retracting into position. She grabbed Ashley's arm. "No, wait! Where are you going?"

"We have to see who you ran over, if we can help!" Ash said, her eyes wide and fearful. Jen felt a cool assessment taking over, giving her enough sense to wonder why her sister was so upset. She wasn't the one in the driver's seat, after all. *I'm going to jail.*

When the car door opened, the sound of rain deafened her. She watched as Ashley got out of the car, unworried about getting wet. Drops ricocheted off the car door to spray haphazardly on Jen's face. She blinked and wiped them away, opening her eyes to see that Ashley hadn't bothered to shut the door behind her. Annoyance trickled through the numbness.

Jen switched off the car engine and unclicked

her own belt, letting it slide along her palm into its housing. With trepidation she opened her own door and stepped out, immediately drenched. When the car door slammed shut Jen looked for her sister, seeing her nowhere.

"Ash?" she called. "Ashley!"

"Oh no," Ash wailed from the opposite side of the car. Across the roof Jen saw nothing and knew that Ash must be on her hands and knees, looking under the car. *Do I really want to see this?*

Compelled beyond understanding, Jen crouched. Her jeans stuck awkwardly to her, forcing her to shuffle and pull up the material of each leg before she could bend further and peer under the car. The first thing she saw was Ashley's face on the other side. Her gaze shifted. Close to the back wheel on Ashley's side was a shaggy animal. A dog. *Not a person.*

Jen felt both relief and guilt at once.

She spoke to her sister across the undercarriage. "Why was it running around in the rain? Is it a stray?" She could hear the hopeful tone in her voice and wondered why it mattered less that it had no owner. A dead dog was a dead dog either way, right? *Strays can bite kids. Strays are pests. Strays get put down.*

Her thoughts didn't make her feel any better.

"I can't see a collar," Ashley said, bobbing her

head back and forth.

"Can you move it? I don't want to run over it with the back wheels." The memory of the car thudding over it made her gag.

"Oh my god, Jen. It might just be wounded."

"Even more reason to get it out from under there," Jen insisted.

"I don't want to get bitten," Ashley said.

"Don't be such a wimp. It's probably dead, anyway."

"Then *you* do it!" Ashley snapped. "You're the one who ran it over."

And there it was, thrown in her face. Anger stuttered her mind, making her scramble for a retort. Ashley didn't wait for a reply, getting to her feet so that Jen was left staring at her sneakered feet. Jen stood up straight to yell at her.

"It's on *your* side!"

"So? Walk around!" Ash snapped back. She got back into the passenger seat and shut the door.

Jen's mouth opened in her indignance. She'd just had her first car accident with a fatality and her sister wasn't being supportive. Or nice.

Jen opened the driver's side door and hopped in as well, squelching as she sat behind the wheel. She glared at Ashley. Her sister had retrieved her phone to send a bunch of quick texts.

"Who are you texting?"

"I'm letting mum know what happened."

"You mean letting her have your side of the story," Jen snarked.

Ashley pulled a face at her. "What the hell is wrong with you?"

The question must have been rhetorical because Ash resumed her texting.

With a trembling voice, Jen gave her command. "You get the dog out from under the car, or we're not going anywhere."

Ash threw her a different expression, this one of contempt. "You're not serious."

"I've never been more serious," Jen replied triumphantly.

She would pay for this in one way or another because her sister would find a way to get back at her. But right now she wanted that dog moved out from under the car and she didn't even want to look at it, never mind touch it.

"You're such a shit," Ash complained, but she threw open her car door and stepped out.

"And shut the door!" Jen yelled over the rain.

Ashley turned and that was when the van hit her. Jen blinked her shock as screeching brakes sounded over the pouring rain.

"No, no, no, no, no," she said through a dry

mouth. *That didn't just happen.*

Ashley's phone on her seat blooped, catching her attention. Her mother had texted back.

'I'm so sorry. Just be careful getting it off the road.'

EYE OF THE CROW

The garden was quiet except for the soft rustle of leaves and the cawing of a single crow perched on the wrought-iron gate. Bonnie adjusted her apron, glancing over her shoulder at the kitchen window to ensure no one was watching.

"Come on now, love," she said sweetly. "Time to feed your birdie friends, isn't it? Got a whole bag of breadcrumbs just for them."

The little girl hesitated, clutching a tin pail to

her chest. She was small, her white pinafore spotless against the deep green of the manicured hedges. Her dark eyes studied Bonnie with an intensity that made her throat tighten.

"They're not hungry yet," the girl said.

"Course they're hungry. Birds're always hungry, darlin'. Come on, let's go to the grove." Bonnie reached for the girl's hand, resisting the urge to snatch it. Rushing now would spook her.

The girl looked down at her pail, then back up at Bonnie. Something about her gaze—too calm, too knowing—sent a prickle down Bonnie's spine. She smiled through it, her grip tightening.

"Let's go," Bonnie urged.

The girl finally nodded, her movements precise. They walked together, her small hand nestled in Bonnie's, past the rose bushes and the statue of a marble angel with its arms outstretched. Another crow landed on the fountain, watching.

They were nearly at the grove when Clyde stepped out from behind the oak. He was tall, broad-shouldered, his denim jacket patched at the elbows. His face was rough-hewn, unshaven, but his eyes gleamed with purpose.

"Right, then," Clyde said, his voice low and steady. He had a burlap sack in his hands.

Bonnie crouched, gripping the girl's

shoulders. "Don't scream, love," she whispered, her breath warm against the child's ear. "This'll all be over soon."

The girl tilted her head, as though considering Bonnie's words, before giving a small nod. She did not scream when Clyde swept her into the sack. The tin pail clattered to the ground, scattering breadcrumbs across the moss.

Bonnie glanced around the garden one last time. The crows on the gate and the fountain were still watching, their black eyes glinting like beads. She shivered before hurrying after Clyde.

The hideout was a ramshackle cabin on the outskirts of town, hidden behind a tangle of trees and vines. It had once been a hunter's lodge, but now smelt of mildew and stale tobacco. Clyde set down the burlap sack onto the battered sofa, before putting his back to the nearby wall.

"Well, that was easy," he said, pulling a cigarette from his pocket. He lit it with a flick of his lighter, the flame dancing briefly in the dim room. "Kid's quiet as a mouse. I was expecting some screaming, maybe a little kicking. Hell, I'd even take some tears."

Bonnie pulled off her apron and threw it onto

the rickety table. "Told you she's not like other kids," she muttered, brushing her hands down her skirt. "She gives me the creeps."

Clyde smirked, blowing a stream of smoke toward the cracked ceiling. "Oh, come on. You're scared of a six-year-old? Ain't she the reason we're gonna be rolling in cash soon?"

Bonnie glanced at the sack, where the girl was eerily still. She had expected muffled cries or at least some movement, but the fabric barely shifted. She grabbed the mouth of the sack and yanked it down.

The girl unfolded herself to sit cross-legged on the sofa, and watched them with dark eyes. Her hands were neatly folded in her lap, and her pinafore was as spotless as it had been in the garden.

"Hello," she said.

Clyde barked out a laugh. "Look at her! Not a care in the world. Bet she thinks this is some kinda game."

Bonnie frowned, crossing her arms. She didn't want to talk in front of the kid but there was nowhere else to go. "She's weird, Clyde. Always has been. Quiet, too polite, like she's not really a kid at all. Look at how she stares. Like she's trying to figure out what makes us tick."

Clyde took another drag of his cigarette.

"Better this than bawling her head off. Makes our job easier, don't it?"

Bonnie didn't answer. She couldn't shake the unease creeping up her spine. The girl's gaze was locked on her now, steady and unblinking.

Clyde tossed his cigarette onto the floorboards, grinding it out with his boot. "Right, let's talk payday. You left the note, right?"

Bonnie nodded curtly. "On the dining table."

"Tomorrow morning, I'll pick up the cash. Then we figure out what to do with her."

Bonnie stiffened. "What do you mean, what to do with her? We're giving her back."

"Are we?" Clyde raised an eyebrow. "She's seen our faces. Your fake name when you worked there will only get you so far. Hell, she's probably memorised everything about us."

"You're not talking about—"

"I'm talking about staying free," Clyde interrupted, his tone icy. "If we don't handle this right, her daddy's gonna come after us with everything he's got. And trust me, people like him don't stop looking."

Bonnie glanced at the girl again. She was still watching, her expression serene, as if the conversation wasn't about her at all.

"We don't... do *that*... to kids," Bonnie said firmly. "We're not monsters, Clyde."

"And if we let her go, we're done," Clyde shot back. "Think about it."

Bonnie's jaw tightened, but she said nothing. The girl finally broke her gaze, turning her head toward the window. Outside, the caw of a crow echoed through the stillness.

The bathroom was small and dingy, its single window crusted with grime. The mirror above the chipped sink reflected a faint, hazy image of the little girl as she stood on tiptoe to reach the faucet. The water ran cold and sluggish, dripping over her hands as she splashed her face.

"Don't take all day in there," Bonnie called from outside. "You've got two minutes."

The girl ignored her, drying her hands on the threadbare towel.

Tap. Tap. Tap.

A crow perched on the windowsill, its head cocked to one side. Its beady black eyes met hers through the dirty glass. It tapped its beak against the pane again, harder this time, as if urging her to come closer.

The girl climbed onto the toilet seat with deliberate movements, her small hands testing the rusted latch on the window. It groaned as she pushed, the glass grinding in its tracks. The gap was narrow—barely wide enough to let in the night air—but the crow didn't fly away. It simply fluttered its wings at the window's movement, its head tilting as she leant close.

She pressed her mouth to the opening, her voice a soft whisper. "I need help. Please."

The crow cawed sharply in reply. Beyond the window, the shadows of the trees stirred, the leaves rustling like whispers carried on the wind. Another caw answered from somewhere deeper in the night.

The girl climbed back down. Bonnie banged on the door. "Time's up, kid! Let's go."

The girl opened the door and stepped out. Bonnie's lips were pressed into a thin line. She grabbed the girl by the shoulder, steering her back to the sofa where Clyde sat, flipping through a magazine.

"Well?" Clyde asked, barely looking up.

"She's fine," Bonnie snapped, shoving the girl toward the sofa. "Happy now?"

Clyde smirked. "Still quiet as a mouse. We lucked out with this one."

The girl sat down, her hands folded neatly in her lap, her legs crossed at the ankles. Her dark eyes flicked briefly toward the window before settling on the floor. Outside, the faint rustle of leaves grew louder, punctuated by the occasional caw of a crow.

Neither Bonnie nor Clyde seemed to notice.

Morning seeped into the cabin through thin curtains, weak and pale. Bonnie sat at the table, cradling a mug of lukewarm coffee, her eyes locked on Clyde. He was pacing, the floorboards creaking under his boots, a cigarette hanging from his lips.

"I'll go get the ransom," Clyde said, his tone leaving no room for debate. "You stay here with the kid."

Bonnie scoffed. "Oh, sure. Let you take all the money and run? Not a chance."

Clyde stopped mid-step, turning to face her. "Don't start with me, Bon. This whole thing was your idea, remember? Now you don't trust me?"

Bonnie's jaw tightened. "It's not about trust, Clyde. It's about common sense. You think I don't know you'd bolt the second that cash hits your hands?"

Clyde smirked, but there was no humour in it. "And what about you? Leave me here with her, and next thing I know, you're on a train south with the loot."

Bonnie set her mug down with a loud clunk, leaning forward. "We're partners. I didn't drag you into this just so you could screw me over."

"Partners don't look at each other like they're holding knives," Clyde muttered, stubbing out his cigarette in a chipped ashtray. "I'm the one who knows how to scope out the drop-off point without being seen. So I'm going."

The girl sat quietly on the sofa, her small frame swallowed by its tattered cushions. Her dark eyes shifted between Bonnie and Clyde.

Bonnie noticed her gaze and shuddered. "Look, why don't we both go? Tie her up. She's not going anywhere."

Clyde frowned. "You want to leave her alone? What if someone stumbles by?"

Bonnie threw up her hands. "Who's going to come out here, Clyde? This place is a dump."

The girl finally spoke, her voice soft and measured. "You don't have to argue. My father will pay for me. It'll be over soon."

Both Bonnie and Clyde turned to her, startled by the sudden interjection. Clyde scowled and looked away, but Bonnie couldn't shake the strange feeling her words gave her.

"All right," Clyde said after a moment, grabbing his jacket from the back of a chair. "We tie her up, then we both go. No funny business,

Bonnie. I'll be watching."

Together, they bound the girl's wrists and ankles with rope, securing her to a wooden chair. She didn't resist, her expression as calm as ever.

When they were done, Clyde opened the door to leave. A crow immediately flew in, its black wings brushing his face. "What the—" he growled, swatting at the bird as it circled the room.

"Get it out of here!" Bonnie snapped, ducking as it swooped toward her.

"Hold on," Clyde muttered, stepping back inside and slamming the door shut. The crow landed on the table, cocking its head as it looked at him.

"Damn thing's mocking me," Clyde said, his voice low and angry. He raised his hand to swat it away.

Before he could, a loud caw sounded from outside, followed by another, and another. Bonnie froze, her eyes darting toward the window. Shadows passed the windows, black shapes flitting and gathering.

"What's going on?" she whispered.

The crow on the table cawed again, louder this time, almost triumphant. Then, like a storm breaking, the air filled with deafening caws and the sound of wings battering against the door and windows.

Clyde stared at the door as if hypnotized, his hand still raised mid-swat. "That's a lot of birds," he said, his voice almost drowned out by the growing cacophony.

Windows smashed, and the hurricane arrived.

Crows poured in like a black tide, their wings filling the room, claws scratching at everything, beaks pecking and tearing. Bonnie screamed, trying to shield her face, but they swarmed her. Clyde swung wildly, shouting, but the birds overwhelmed him.

The girl sat perfectly still, her eyes closed, listening to the chaos. The caws were deafening, mingling with the frantic screams of Bonnie and Clyde. She didn't flinch, even as feathers brushed her face, and the ropes around her wrists and ankles were pecked at, slowly loosening.

When the cabin fell silent, she opened her eyes.

The floor was littered with feathers, blood, and the unmoving bodies of Bonnie and Clyde. Crows perched everywhere—in the rafters, on the table, along the back of the sofa. One stepped forward and pecked the last knot of rope until it fell away.

The girl stood, smoothing her pinafore. "Thank you," she said softly.

The crows parted as she walked to the door, stepping over the bodies without a glance. Outside, the morning was calm, the air fresh with the smell of pine. She made her way down the road, her small feet steady on the dirt path, while the crows watched from the treetops, their black eyes gleaming.

The garden was quiet again, golden afternoon light over the rose bushes and the marble angel that watched over the grounds. The rich man stood at the window of his grand estate, hands clasped behind his back and face unreadable as he watched his daughter in the garden below.

She stood by the fountain, a tin pail in one hand and breadcrumbs in the other. Around her, a murder of crows gathered, black bodies dotting the grass like living shadows. They watched her with the same intensity she watched them, her dark eyes meeting theirs in silent communion.

She scattered the breadcrumbs, her movements slow and deliberate. The birds hopped closer. One crow perched on the edge of the fountain, tilting its head to study her. She tilted hers in return, a faint smile curving her lips.

The crows closed in around her, black feathers shining like oil in the sunlight. She reached out a hand, a raven hopping onto her wrist with the ease of familiarity.

The rich man turned away from the window, pulling the curtains shut. Outside, the cawing of the crows rose into the air, sharp and rhythmic, like laughter.

ECHOES OF SOLACE

A familiar noise wakes me. I climb out of bed and sneak along the corridor to the stairs. Clutching the bannister with both hands, I work my way down. The front room is quiet and dark as I hurry to the kitchen. Carpet gives way to cold tiles and I stop. My mother hunches by the open fridge door, bathed in light and eating. I question her and she slams the door shut, causing glass to chink inside. I am shooed to bed and tucked in, and told not to share what I have seen. I promise and go to sleep.

Dressed in black, I look at the coffin and wonder at its size. It looks normal. Surrounding it are large collections of flowers—mostly geraniums, my mother's favourite. People fill the church but nobody says anything to me until my father and I are outside, then everybody offers the same words about how big my mother's heart was. Nobody mentions how big she was.

Dressed in white, I marry a man who I thought would never look twice at me. He is intelligent, successful, and absent. The honeymoon is the longest time I've spent with him, where we made our son together on a golden island. Now the mornings are a rush to get to work and I am in bed before he gets home. On the weekends he is too tired to do anything or go anywhere. I tell him I understand and squash my resentment. I recall our vows, where he promised to provide for me. Nobody promised to spend time together.

As the house sleeps, I prowl. Tightening my dressing gown with white knuckled fists, I enter the kitchen. Cupboard door hinges squeak and a packet is furtively opened before I approach my true objective; the fridge. Behind jars of jams and sauces is a container of dip. I pry the lid open and peel back the foil seal before sinking chip after chip, making them disappear one and then two at a time. Salty, creamy goodness satisfies my cravings. I cast a guilty eye on the empty container and bury my arm into the rubbish bin, hiding the evidence. The lid closes with a clang and I hear the baby stirring. I hurry to his room but he has dozed off before sounding the alarm.

After my husband goes to work, I clean. Floors are mopped and vacuumed and the washing is on the line. I have a reward waiting for me. Like a nervous schoolgirl I approach the fridge and open the door, staring at its contents. Feel-good promises scream at me from every colourful tub, packet and bottle. I find my treasure and unwrap it, engulfing multiple rows of chocolate at a time. The packet says 'family size' but I am the only one here. I throw away the wrapping and by the time my son comes home from school, there appears to be only a wad of paper towels in the bin.

My husband won't look at me even though he is across the boardroom table. I try to close my jacket over my ample bosom but it won't reach. I look at the pen I am holding, its streamlined design a juxtaposition of my plump hand. With a flourish, I sign my name on a document that makes me single again—and also very well off. He has thrown money at me so he can marry his yoga instructor without fuss. I don't believe I'll notice a difference in my life. On the way home I stop at a supermarket and replenish supplies for the house. To celebrate the end of an era, I throw in a few extra treats.

At home while I am getting an after-dinner snack, my son asks if he can stay over at a friend's house. I look at him, at his young teenage self—he has five years to go before he is a man. I could say no, keep him with me, spend time with him. Perhaps we could play one of his computer games together, there's one that I'm good at—something to do with platforms. When he prompts for my answer, I am reminded of a long-forgotten moment in time—of my mother bathed in the glow of the fridge light as I waited for her attention.

I shut the fridge door harshly enough to make glass bottles chink inside.

FADE

The constant murmur of conversations were punctuated by sounds of clinking glass and cutlery on china. Light classical music poured from discreetly placed speakers and added to the background noise. Through large plate windows the city twinkled beyond the famous opera house and the harbour where it sat. I was taking a sip of water when Claire brought up a name that struck me as vaguely familiar.

"Did anybody find out what happened to Lisa Griffin?" she asked.

"Was she an actress in something?" Tom didn't look up when he spoke, focussed on buttering his bread to the very edges. I watched his process with mute fascination, the way he swept his knife back and forth, using both sides of it to butter.

"What? No, she went to our high school. She was in our year." Claire explained, wine glass in hand. Her fingers pinched it by the stem. I recalled a wine tour some years ago that I'd taken with a boyfriend at the time, listening to a sommelier explain that a glass of wine should never be held by the bowl, because fingers changed the temperature.

Rick nodded and joined the conversation. "Oh yeah, she was the captain of the debate team."

He was wrong. I'd participated in debating and Lisa Griffin hadn't been a part of that, although she should have. "You're thinking of Samantha Hartley." I knew who Claire meant, helped into the memory by the context of her question. "Lisa Griffin was the girl who went missing halfway through our final year."

Tom's knife paused midway through a stroke so he could look first at Claire, then at me. The intensity of his dark-eyed gaze penetrated me to the bone. "I remember hearing about it on the news, but she didn't go to our school."

"No," Claire said slowly, pulling Tom's stare back to her. I felt a relief when it went, but I also wished it had stayed. Claire swirled her wine, and I watched as the viscosity of the red liquid left a trace on the glass wherever it touched. "She went to our school. I was on the swim team with her."

Tom refocussed on his bread. He finished buttering and bit into it, knife still in hand.

I took the opportunity to extend the conversation. I hadn't thought about Lisa Griffin at all after leaving high school. When at university, I didn't have time to think about anything beyond my studies. It had been a struggle, but with perseverance I'd achieved my diploma.

"She wanted to be a lawyer," I said. I'd had exactly one conversation with Lisa Griffin throughout my entire school experience, and it had been about our mutual interest. "But she wanted to go into environmental law so she ended up joining that recycling group. What were they called?"

"Waste Warriors," Rick said, and laughed like he'd heard a hilarious joke. After a moment of solitary humour, he realised he was on his own and his chuckles petered out. I watched him take a sip of his beer and wondered how long he and Claire would last. They'd hooked up at the ten-year reunion last week. He was extremely good-looking but didn't appear to share many of Claire's interests or life experiences. Claire was culturally intelligent, having travelled every continent, including Antarctica. She'd been an adventurer as long as I'd known her, since primary school.

"I remember that group. They organised for recycling bins to be placed around the school," Tom said, looking up. Because I was seated opposite him, we made eye contact. I smiled, feeling self-conscious as my mind cast about for something to say. Rick beat me to it.

"I saw them bin diving. I hope they were as passionate about baths as they were about bottles," Rick said, laughing even as he made his statement. Or joke. Or whatever that was supposed to be. My gaze returned to Tom.

"I think I remember her," he told me, like I was the one who'd brought her up. "Was she a dark blonde that always wore her hair in a high ponytail?"

I nodded and my hand went to my hair, which was down. I fiddled with a lock of it, surprised Tom noticed things like that. Most men barely remember the colour, let alone how a girl wore it. It made me think perhaps he'd noticed her because he'd liked her. A bolt of envy trickled into my soul and I shunned it; seriously, I was jealous of a girl who was probably long dead?

"I've not thought about her since after high school," I confessed.

"Same," Tom said. His answer pleased me more than it should have. He returned his attention to his plate and I wondered how I could compete with steak.

"Didn't they find her body or something?" I asked. "Years later, maybe?"

"No, I don't think anybody found anything," Claire said. I watched her stare lower to the phone on the table to the right side of her plate, screen face down. There was a pause as she considered the rudeness of picking it up.

"Go on, let's see who can google it quicker," I said, taking my mobile out of my jacket pocket. Claire giggled and we both lapsed into silence. I ran a few different searches using her name, our school, adding the term 'missing' but there was nothing. I scrolled and frowned and scrolled some more.

"It's like she doesn't exist," Claire murmured, obviously getting the same results.

"Really? Nothing?" Rick asked. He was on his

phone next. "Did you try adding her name with our school?"

Tom snorted. "I'm quite sure these two are smart enough to have thought of that." I offered him a tiny smile and it broke into a grin when he winked at me. My stomach flipped and I put my phone back in my jacket pocket, Lisa Griffin once again forgotten.

I thought about her one more time after that, after we left the restaurant and just before Tom's hand reached for mine as we walked towards the train station. I thought about Lisa Griffin and the brief impact she'd had on our lives. I remembered her as vivacious and passionate, pretty and filled with so much potential. I remember watching her crying parents on television, pleading for her whereabouts, for her to come home.

I felt sad for her, that the world moved on and that she, as a human being, was whittled down to nothing more than a story attached to 'whatever happened to'? That she would fade, so completely, into nothing at all.

STARCROSSED

The pair lay intertwined on synthetic grass softer than cotton. With her head cushioned in the valley of his shoulder, Rosaline admired the stars. They were white glowing pixels in the imperfect black screen of space. Her cheek registered the shift of his muscles before fingertips caressed her arm, causing fine hairs to rise.

"We're meant to be together," Romeo

whispered. Rosaline coughed a sigh. "We *are*," he insisted.

"I'm not with you just because my father approves," she scorned.

"Openly, you mean."

Rosaline didn't know what he meant. She didn't want to ask for clarification because it would lead to a complaint. Romeo was a gorgeous young man with a romantic soul, but the latter made him barely tolerable. His mouth was more useful to her when it wasn't talking.

"Don't ruin the moment," she chastised, wriggling in his hold to remind him of why they'd come here.

"The moment is already lost," he said mournfully.

"FFS," she said while sitting up, the trio of letters saving her from attracting a profanity fine. She didn't want to push her luck after her father had paid the last lot, amounting to tens of thousands of credits. Pocket change for an affluent man but she didn't want to have another argument about it so soon after the last one.

"Don't be angry because I want more than sex from you," he pleaded.

She hugged her knees and pushed down her guilt, hating that he loved her so much. For them to possess a contractual union was the hope of many—but especially her father, who'd mentioned Romeo's eligibility to her many times. Romeo only enhanced such wishes when countless holo-flowers and digi-grams arrived daily. She would throw them into recycling and wonder what would become of them. A graveyard in the cloud.

She couldn't be with him. As much as she was attracted to him (and even though the tragic poet in him exasperated her, there were worse flaws in men)—she knew she didn't love him. She barely tolerated him. She'd been born into a life of meeting others' expectations and didn't want to marry into it as well. Romeo wasn't controlling like her father was, but he could be influenced. It was sometimes his saving grace.

"It doesn't get easier," she murmured.

"What doesn't?" he asked, reaching for her hand before she could pull it away.

"Relationships. There's no formula for them. No clear answers. They rely on illogical emotion and they're unpredictable."

"It's always been that way. Why would it get easier?"

Rosaline turned to look at Romeo in surprise. Sometimes, even with his melancholy, he could turn up gems. She wondered if she was being too hard on him.

No. He was insufferable.

"Let's just enjoy this moment," he pleaded, perhaps knowing that their time would soon come to an end.

She lay beside him once more, beneath a projected sky.

TEN THOUSAND REASONS

I wake up alone.

The mattress beside me is warm and the sheets are crumpled, the scene of a quick getaway. The room is dark but daylight peeks through the imperfections of my blinds, giving dust-motes a stage upon which to dance. I want to enjoy the moment, but it feels like someone has spooned out my insides.

I stumble out of bed and make my way to the

bathroom, leaving sweaty handprints on the walls. I flick up the lid of the toilet seat and it hits the tank with a clunk. I double over the bowl and wait for the heaving to begin. Nothing comes. Habit compels me to flush, and I smell the cloying, artificial scent of lavender that emanates from the plastic doodad attached beneath the seat.

My phone chirps a familiar sound, one that causes a flutter of excitement throughout my body. With one hand on my stomach like an expectant mother, I quick-step to my bedside table and unplug my phone. The movement causes its screen to glow, and I tap on the most recent email.

The sender is mellon_collie using an online email service. I already don't like my newest client. Their username has too many personal clues. They're a Smashing Pumpkins fan. They enjoy 90s alternative rock. They own that album. They're most likely a Generation X.

To spite myself, I open the email. The code phrase is the only thing in the message.

I have ten thousand reasons to leave.

My phone highlights my satisfied smile in the dark, like a teller of ghost stories.

I arrange a place and time to meet. I choose a public park at ten in the morning. It's a popular location for joggers and mothers with strollers. Sometimes the two even combine. I sit on a park bench with the sun at my back, facing a fountain. Tourists wanting a good photo won't aim the camera my way.

Because I don't have a baby, I'm dressed as a jogger. A water bottle at my side complements my leggings and zip-up hoodie. Wearing sunglasses and with my dark hair pulled back into a high ponytail, I'm barely noticed. I see my client long before she sees me.

I should get up and jog away, leaving her clueless and abandoned. Against my self-interest, I wait until she notices me. My water bottle's green and white stripes are distinctive, and she knows to look for it.

She makes her way over as I sit upright and I wonder how the hell she even found me. This woman, this mellon_collie, isn't the hardened criminal I usually deal with. She's the kind of person who would adopt a pet from the animal shelter.

She is unconventionally bad at being discreet. Wearing a polka dot scarf over her hair and oversized shades on her face, she looks like something out of a retro movie; something starring Monroe or Hepburn. When she sits beside me, she places a giant handbag on the seat between us and rifles through it while talking. Maybe she saw this in a movie. It must've been a comedy.

"I'm the one who sent you the email," she says.

I reach into the pocket of my hoodie and pull out a folded note. It's small, half the size of a post-it. On it are the details of a bank account to a burner business I have.

"Take this." I hold out the note and she snatches it from between my fingers. When she looks at it, I give her the rest of my instructions. "After you give me your ten thousand reasons, I'll send you an address where we can meet up."

"And you'll help me disappear?" Her tone is soft and hopeful, and I frown at her while she buries my note deep inside her bag.

"Nobody will ever find you," I promise. I pull my feet in to stand, but she puts a hand on my arm, stopping me.

"I... I can only give you four thousand dollars," she whispers.

"You said you had ten thousand reasons." My voice is firm. The terms are non-negotiable.

"I do!" A furtive glance has her dropping her voice even though nobody looked our way. "I have reasons, actual reasons for leaving. My husband, he'll end up killing me if I stay. He'll hunt me down if I leave."

I'm horrified. *This* is why she wanted my help? She doesn't want to go where I'd be taking her; she doesn't have any idea what she's really asking. Knowing her reason means I wouldn't help her even if she had the money. She needs to know I'm a closed door.

"That's only one reason," I say coldly. "I'm not a charity."

"But I can't ask anyone else for help. I need you. He's a cop."

Her last word causes chills to travel down my arms and legs, yet my face feels hot. I become hyperaware of my breathing. This woman is a threat to my lifestyle, and I need to get away from her. I surge to my feet and walk away like a robot that needs oiling in its joints.

"Please!" she cries at my back, a forlorn bleating from a dying lamb. I cannot save her, and she has put me in jeopardy. My mouth is so dry that when I swallow, I can hear a click. I want to clear my throat but that'll make me conspicuous. Won't it? I break into a jog to take me as far away from the woman as possible.

After a shower, I feel better. Towelling myself dry, I can hear my phone chime the arrival of an email. I take my time before going to it, positive about who the email is from. When I check my phone, I see I'm right. I was right about her being a Gen X, too.

I shouldn't read the email, I should delete it and continue on with my life. I don't need to get involved with this tragedy. I end up opening it.

'Please help me. I can't go to the police because they'll cover for him. He's manipulative and careful and he always covers his tracks. Even our closest friends suspect nothing. I'm trapped with no way out. I've sent you four thousand reasons. Please let that be enough.'

Why am I putting myself through this heartache? I reply to her message with four simple words: 'Don't contact me again'. I delete her messages and mine before checking my bank account. Yes, there's her payment, stupid woman. She should've kept that money and used it to buy a plane ticket to the other side of the world. People disappear all the time. She doesn't need what I'm selling.

It's a week later when I get a new client. When I

meet him, I'm not surprised to see who it is. He's got his fingers in all kinds of criminal pies and he's in currently in the papers in relation to a killing. The victim has suspected mob ties, so he'll be an easy target in jail if the court case doesn't go his way… if he even makes it to court.

His money is in my account and I'm waiting for him to show up. I don't worry about him knowing where I live, not when I'm going to be helping him disappear. It will be a few hours before he's supposed to get here, so I pass the time curled up on the sofa with a book. Reading is the best way to keep myself calm before a client arrives, otherwise I will pace and overthink.

A knock at my door surprises me. It's possibly the client, too anxious about disappearing to wait until our designated meeting time. That's happened a few times before. When I open the door, there's a man I don't recognise on the other side of it.

"Hayley Etheridge?" he says. Hearing my name gives me a peculiar sensation in my stomach, like I'm about to receive bad news. Nobody has said my name in a long time.

"Yeah?" I prompt, wondering if this is perhaps a new building manager. I bought the penthouse using my real identity. It's better to leave some trace of yourself for tax purposes. If I didn't exist at all, that would raise suspicions.

He flashes a badge at me and steps forward into my apartment, even though I'm standing in the doorway. I'm forced to yield lest I get pushed back. I don't want a physical altercation because that might lead to something worse.

Instead of yelling at him to get out, I ask him politely, "What's going on? Is somebody in trouble?"

I hope it's not me.

"You could say that." His smile seems genuine but is not reassuring. Who smiles after forcing their way into a person's residence?

"Are you here to ask questions?" I prompt, wanting to keep this interaction peaceful. I don't know who he is or why he's here yet, so I want him to feel like he has the upper hand, like he's in control. After dealing with so many criminals, I've learnt that challenges only create a hostile environment primed for violence.

"I do have questions," he says, moving farther into my apartment. He glances at the huge artwork upon the lounge room wall, passes the three-piece leather suite and stops to stare out the floor-to-ceiling windows that look out over the river. "How does a twenty-four-year-old woman that freelances as an I.T. consultant afford to buy a place like this?" The way he casually drops information makes me realise he's been investigating me for a while. Was it because he spotted me with a high-profile criminal? I don't think that's it. He's here on his own. A case like that would require a partner.

"I'm good at what I do," I say, moving beside him. "I'm lucky to have a lot of clients who trust me."

He has the advantage of knowing who I am, but he doesn't have details. How could he? I'm pretty sure I know who he is and why he's here. I wouldn't call that knowledge an advantage, though.

"Such as?" he asks.

We both know I don't have I.T. clients.

"I'm sorry, I've signed non-disclosure agreements with all of them."

"And did you sign an NDA with my wife as well?" he asks. I can see his anger beneath the surface, swirling and bubbling. I see it in his posture and the way he's looking at me.

"Your wife?" I ask, because I don't have mellon_collie's name.

"Michelle Ballard," he grinds. "And don't play dumb."

I give him something closer to the truth. "Okay, I don't work in I.T., but that's only because my clients would be embarrassed about it."

There is vindication in his eyes and a triumphant smile on his face. He got information out of me using intimidation tactics. As long as he feels he's winning, I can get out of this.

"Tell me," he says gruffly. He selects my armchair to sit in while I perch on the sofa. I want to run away, but this is the kind of man who would hunt me down. That's what his wife said.

I hope she's alright.

The way he glares at me lets me know I should start talking. "I have the ability to take people into my dreams with me."

"What?" he asks, the question spat out as a statement of incredulity.

"It's something I've always been able to do. Anyone who falls asleep with me shares my dream. I become their spiritual guide." I give him a sweet smile while I pour it on thick. "There are many people who want to experience genuine psychic phenomena and that's how I make my money. I charge ten thousand dollars a go."

"Ten thousand?" he repeats. I remember Michelle only sent me four.

"Michelle asked for a discount. It was a slow month, so I allowed it." The lie comes smoothly and I embellish it with some truth. "She hasn't come here to go on a dream yet."

I wonder if he'll ask for a refund or if he's curious enough about what I do to go in her place. Honestly, I don't care which option he chooses if it gets him out of my life. I wonder about the time, if I have long before my client shows. If he comes here while a policeman is in my penthouse, I will lose the bit of control I have.

"Why would Michelle even care about this psychic shit?" His words are rough but I can see doubt in him.

"I'm sorry, I can't tell you that. But I can tell you that every one of my clients have a life-changing experience when they dream with me."

"What happens if they don't? Do they get a refund?"

My stomach flops with excitement instead of nerves. My smile brightens with anticipation. "Of course. Nobody has ever asked for a refund, though." I say this proudly because I've never had to return money.

He scoffs but I can see a glimmer of his interest. "How do you do it? Through meditation?"

"No, we both need to be asleep," I say. "If someone can't get to sleep, we use sleeping pills."

"I'm not taking sleeping pills," he says sharply.

"You don't have to. Would you like to try

falling asleep without them?" I stand and step close to him so I can offer my hand. He looks at me like I'm insane but he takes my hand and stands. His palms are chafed and dry. I dislike touching him but I can't show fear.

"And what do you do while I'm trying to fall asleep?" he asks. His tone has shifted dramatically, which means he no longer sees me as a threat.

"I'll be falling asleep beside you," I say. "I'll probably end up sleeping first as I've had more practise than you." I laugh softly but it's true. This will hopefully make him trust me the rest of the way.

"Alright, I'll try it."

I lead him to my darkened bedroom.

"We're doing this on your bed?" he asks through a smile.

"Yes," I say. I don't think he believes me, that we're going to dream together. I think he considers this to be my roundabout way of bribing him with sex. Whatever he thinks doesn't matter as long as he doesn't act on it.

I let go of his hand to sit on the bed on my side. When he sits on the opposite side, I lay down atop the covers. He does the same. We go through some breathing exercises together and then we both lie silently, breathing and focussing on nothing but falling asleep.

I feel myself drift off.

When I open my eyes, I'm in the other world, the place I go to when I sleep. I'm standing on a rocky outcrop on the side of a barren mountain. In the distance, I can see a silvery ocean. Below me on the plains is a herd of large bear-like creatures. After a few minutes of waiting, I sense another presence nearby and I turn and see the policeman.

He is open-mouthed, staring first at me and then at the world I have brought him to.

"This... this is amazing," he says, then looks up at the sky. "That's impossible."

I look up as well, knowing that I will see two faded moons in the violet sky. I don't know if we're on another planet in a distant solar system that I access through my dream or if it's another dimension, but it doesn't matter.

"Your wife wanted to escape to this place," I say. He's barely listening, too interested in what he can see around him. "She wanted me to leave her here to get away from you."

"She what?" he asks, his brow furrowing. I have his attention now.

"But I couldn't do that to her. This place, it's treacherous. She probably wouldn't have cared, but I couldn't do that to her. Because I don't know if this world still exists when I wake up or if it resets itself."

"Don't you talk about my wife," he warns, pointing an accusatory finger my way. I can hear something different in his voice again; he's scared. I'm sure that's a new sensation for him.

"See those?" I say, pointing at the herd. "They look placid, but I've seen them chase down their prey. You don't want to be near them, that's for sure." I'm doing him a favour, telling him about them, but I don't think it'll help in the long run.

I watch as he looks down at them and I wonder if he can see how powerful they are. I liken them to grizzlies, but they're a bit bigger than that.

"And there's this thing that burrows under sand. It looks kind of like a cuttlefish except it's human sized. I wouldn't mess with that, either." I laugh at his expression.

"Why would anyone pay you money to come here?" he asks. "After we wake up, you're giving my money back."

I smile at him and move to the edge of the outcrop. It's a long drop to the ground from here.

"You weren't listening before, but that's okay,

I can say it more simply. Your wife paid me to escape to this place, because that's what I really do. I help people disappear. They all end up coming here, to this world. It's a one-way ticket, buddy. There isn't any going back, for you."

I leap off the outcrop while the policeman curses behind me. With the wind roaring in my ears, I am falling to my death, but I never hit the ground.

I wake up, alone.

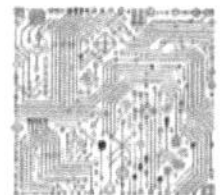

ANOTHER STATE OF BEING

"Today's the day I change," Berrick said, his voice wavering with excitement as he approached his friends. Nervous energy poured off him, infecting those in the waiting room. A woman with greying hair seated nearby started clapping, but nobody else joined her applause. She stopped and clasped her hands tightly on her lap.

Berrick's two buddies who'd come with him for emotional support, got to their feet. Lanter vigorously shook Berrick's hand. Myro gave a tight smile, but the micro-expression on his face a moment ago had been vastly different. He watched as the two young men eagerly discussed Berrick's upcoming transformation. There were no breaks in the conversation until Lanter suggested they help Berrick organise his personal belongings for collection.

"It's quite sudden, don't you think?" Myro asked, glancing from Berrick to Lanter and back again when they both gave him the same confused look. "I mean, most people change after they turn fifty." Myro gestured at the senior looking lady who'd clapped. She'd either sensed their attention or overheard his comment because she looked their way and shook her head.

"Rude. I'm forty-nine, not fifty."

Myro wanted to continue prompting for Berrick to use his logic as they exited the waiting room and moved down the corridors of the government building. The echoes of their footfalls joined many others as people headed for various departments.

Myro didn't want his opinions overheard because they weren't socially acceptable, though not illegal. He waited until they were past the security gate and headed down the wide stone steps. "Shouldn't you at least try for an appeal?

There's a reason the Tribunal exists."

Berrick scoffed at Myro's concern. He looked to Lanter walking on his other side and gestured towards Myro with a 'do you believe this guy' expression on his face. Lanter took this as his cue to defend Berrick's position.

"The Tribunal is a figurehead to calm the masses. They don't actually do anything. They're *people*."

They reached the bottom of the stairs and waited for a big enough gap in the moving walkway to fit all three of them. Once they grabbed the railing and stepped on, Myro turned back to Berrick.

"You're not even thirty, yet. You're not ready for a transmigration."

"Relax, Myro. His number came up like anybody else. Are you jealous, or something?" Lanter's tone shifted into something Myro recognised and didn't like. There were many facets of Lanter's personality that he overlooked to keep the peace between them. They were both Berrick's friend, but not friends with one another.

"Your number shouldn't have come up at all," Myro insisted. "The algorithm got it wrong."

A murmur caught his attention and he glanced over his shoulder to see a middle-aged couple on the walkway in front of him. Both men had their mouths downturned in disapproval. Myro looked back to Berrick who was wide-eyed with embarrassment.

"Don't speak against the algorithm," Berrick warned, his voice low.

Myro could see that reason and logic wasn't working so he changed his tactic, appealing to Berrick's emotions instead. "The Tribunal can fix this. Don't you want to fulfil at least *some* of your goals before transmigrating? Didn't you mention a commitment contract with Channe?"

"Channe will understand," Berrick said firmly. He gave Myro a steady look and added, "She cares about me enough to respect my decisions."

Angrily, Myro replied. "But you don't care enough about her not to die!"

The shift in attitude was palpable. Gasps and comments came from the people around them within earshot and Myro watched as two pink spots flared on Berrick's cheeks. He looked shocked but Lanter didn't. The smug smile on his face said enough. Myro had dissolved his friendship with Berrick while attempting to save him.

To avoid any further discomfort, Myro stepped off the moving walkway. He watched as Berrick and Lanter continued on the conveyer, neither of them looking back. Myro challenged those strangers who dared to stare at him with mute criticism. They all turned their gazes away.

Myro sighed and headed for the cabbie ranks. Cabbies were expensive but one of them could take him all the way home, delivering him directly to his door. He would treat himself with some solitude. After a moment he chuckled to himself, the irony not lost. He would be treating himself to a lot of solitude now, after having lost his only friend.

Myro lined up in the queue and shuffled forward until it was his turn to get into one of the driverless vehicles. He spoke his address and confirmed the map location as correct before the cabbie silently moved through the city streets, darting between other vehicles at intersections, never once slowing below sixty clicks an hour.

He was almost all the way home when he received a message directly on his eye-screen. Very few people had access to its code. Hoping it was Berrick, he activated the message immediately, but a different voice filled his transponder.

"There's a meeting tonight at the usual location. You've already missed a couple. Be there."

Empty air filled Myro's senses after the

message was given. He wasn't sure if it had been automated or if Holden had personally called him, spoken it and immediately disconnected. It was Holden's style to have done the latter. They were as ambiguous in their communication as they were in their pronoun. When it came to Holden, one size certainly did not fit all. They were so much of an outlier that the algorithm couldn't even see them, let alone request them for transmigration.

Myro changed the address to a different part of the city and after confirming it with the cabbie, he sat back and watched the scenery change. Urban sprawl gave way to clusters of apartments that gradually trickled out into designated greenspace. At route marker eight-twenty, the cabbie slowed to a stop. Myro palmed the payment screen, and the appropriate amount of credit was withdrawn from his account. The cabbie silently rolled onto the road, crossed lanes and pivoted on the spot before speeding back to the city.

The early afternoon was chillier than Myro anticipated. He shivered and wished he'd dressed more warmly than his regular tunic and calf-length pants. He was walking in circles and hugging himself when the chugging sound of an engine broke the serenity of the forest. A high-set, old-fashioned vehicle that Holden referred to as a 'pickup' blatted a smoky path up the road to him. Upon its arrival it shuddered and trembled with the force of its machinations. Myro tugged on the passenger side door and climbed into the cab.

"What's up? You've never called me into a meeting before," Myro said in lieu of hello. He'd learnt from experience that Holden didn't use or acknowledge greetings. It was hard to read their expression because they wore a patch over their left eye. Rumours abounded that they'd cut out that eye to avoid detection from the algorithm's extensive network.

"This is important," Holden said, their gnarled hands gripping the steering wheel tight. Even though Myro had travelled in the pickup a few times, the thrill of riding in the ancient machine had not yet passed. Holden shifted a bar between them and the vehicle travelled backwards, its engine whining like a frightened dog. With a quick turn of the wheel in front of them, Holden expertly brought the pickup around and headed back down the road in the direction from which they'd come; away from the city.

"Did you discover something about the transmigration machine?" Myro asked once they were travelling off road, traversing down a well-worn forest path.

"Aye."

Myro held onto the small handle above the door, using it as much as he could to offset the bumps. Holden was driving with more speed than usual.

"Are we in a hurry?"

"Everyone's arrived. You're the last one."

Everyone? Myro focussed on studying the path ahead, bracing himself each time there was a deeper gully on the wheel track. Five minutes later they arrived at a dark green warehouse, doing its best to blend into its surrounds even though it was a giant lump of manmade structure in the middle of a natural forest.

When he and Holden entered the warehouse through a side door, Myro saw that 'everyone' was the right description for the people inside. Whenever he'd attended these meetings, there were maybe a dozen people. A lot of the faces would change but it would only be around a dozen at most. Inside this warehouse there were maybe two hundred. He'd not realised how many Holden's words had affected. It felt good to know that so many people shared his opinion of the transmigrations.

Myro moved a few steps into the crowd and stopped, waiting for Holden to take their spot at the podium on a raised timber dais. Once the white-bearded Holden appeared, the rumblings of the crowd softened and stilled. Every person stood transfixed to what the leader of their group was about to say.

"I was wrong."

A few confused mumblings in the crowd before Holden continued.

"The transmigrations do have a purpose. They're not a method of culling the population like we thought. Well, maybe they are, but not with the result we expect. There is no death. Just change."

Holden lost the assembly. Myro's ears cringed from the outroar around him. People were yelling. He caught a few of their words.

"...they must've got to Holden..."

"...they don't know what they're saying..."

"...why are you saying this, Holden? I don't..."

"...you're a liar and a thief and a..."

"Stop! STOP!" Myro moved through the crowd as he shouted his order. A few others repeated his instructions until there were only a few discontented murmurings. "Let's hear what Holden has to say. They'll explain why they think this!"

Within himself Myro hoped that there would be a reason. He wished it with all his might. He hoped that Holden hadn't succumbed to propaganda. Not Holden, please. Not them.

The crowd finally lapsed into silence, though now it came with a tension not felt before.

"We've always believed that the algorithm was programmed by the government to keep the human population in check. That when we're selected for our change, when we go through the transmigration, that it's a trick. We're similar to the athiests of old, who denied the existence of a God, who considered the Bible to be their kind of programming, the kind to keep the population under control. Programming through a book instead of an algorithm."

The murmurs of the crowd grew a little, having heard this sermon before.

"But they couldn't prove anything, because they had to disprove the existence of God. But this is where we differ. We have the algorithm; we know it is real and that its code can be read. I have seen this code. I have *read* it."

The crowd erupted, not with rage this time but with exhilaration. The air felt electric and someone, Myro didn't know who, held tightly onto his hand. The touch was comforting, and he didn't look around to see who it was. Holden had his full attention.

"Everything we've been told is real. The

people the algorithm calls to it end up as *a part of it.* That is the transmigration. We have eternity inside of the metaverse. We become the electricity that runs in the algorithm's veins. We die in the physical sense, but we are converted into the pulses that move our world and make it run."

With sudden intensity, Myro realised the whole truth, and he didn't know why it changed anything.

"*That's* how humans discovered clean, renewable energy?" he yelled, his question repeated down the line until Holden answered it.

"Yes. The code is clear. We transmigrate into electricity, and we become the world's caretakers. If we die naturally, there is nothing for us except to feed the trees. But if transmigrate, we can become so much more."

Applause broke out and Myro was reminded of the elderly woman in the waiting room. His hand was let go and clapping began beside him. He looked around at their elated faces.

Dissatisfaction poured throughout his body. Berrick would meet his untimely end because an algorithm had requested he give his life to it. He inched closer to the warehouse door and slipped out of it. He saw a handful of other people escaping the warehouse to flee down the forest path.

Myro ran after them, his heart pounding in his chest. He caught up to a young woman with short, spiky hair who was sprinting ahead of the group.

"Wait!" he called out, grabbing her arm. "Where are you going?"

She spun around, her eyes wild with fear. "Anywhere but here. They've all gone mad. Don't you see? It's still murder, even if we become energy!"

Myro nodded, feeling a surge of relief that he wasn't alone in his thoughts. "I know. I can't believe Holden bought into this. We need to warn people, to stop the transmigrations."

The woman stared at him in disbelief. "Stop the transmigrations? Are you serious?" She shook her head vehemently. "No, we need to run. They'll come for us now. We know too much."

As if on cue, shouts echoed from the warehouse behind them. "I don't know where to go," Myro said before he sped after the woman.

"Go dark," she threw over her shoulder, before disappearing into the woods.

"I... how?" he said in her absence.

Today wasn't only the day Berrick changed. It was also the day Myro's world changed.

REALITY ADJACENT

Janina often startles me. She has a knack for concealing her approach. When she speaks from inside my room, I flinch. When I cast a wary gaze at her feet, I see white tennis shoes. I don't know what I expected to find. Ninja socks, maybe? Slippers?

I'm about to greet her when a wasp enters the room. I gasp. Stinging and biting insects give me sweaty palms and a racing heart. Janina sees my panic and hurries over to crouch in front of me, taking both my hands in hers.

"The wasp!" The words come out as a whisper, even though it felt like a scream in my chest. Somewhere along the way it lost its power.

"Shh, it's okay. Don't make any sudden moves. It won't hurt you."

Janina smiles at me with sympathetic eyes. I look at our connected hands; hers, young and supple, mine, old and wrinkled. I feel a pinch on my arm and cry out. Janina lets go to shoo the wasp away before it can sting me again.

"Oh dear," Janina says as she stands. "At least you're not allergic." She states it like it's a consolation prize.

I inspect my arm. A spot of blood pools where I've been stung, but it doesn't ache like I expect. Without being asked, Janina fetches a band-aid. I hope she feels guilty.

Later that day I'm picnicking on a rug with friends in the garden. The sky is cloudless, sunny, and warm. Conversation flows around me until I hear a name.

"That Lydia." Barbara's golden hair is pulled back into a high ponytail, and it swings back and forth when she shakes her head. I'm sure she dyes it because it doesn't look natural. "I bet she'll interrupt his game. Poor Brett can't have a moment without her mooning over him. I wish she'd take the hint."

All four of us look towards the greenhouse where Brett is setting up a chessboard. I search the nearby area and find Lydia watching her prospective paramour from one of the garden benches.

"She's perched on the edge of her seat," Grace remarks. "Just like a cat getting ready to pounce. I bet she'll even do that bum wiggling thing before she goes."

I laugh along with everyone else. Lydia hears our amusement and looks our way. I raise my hand to wave, but she pretends not to notice. She sits farther back on the bench, not brave enough to make a move under watchful eyes.

"What a shame. I wanted to see it play out." Mrs Walcott tuts from her wheelchair. On her lap is a small tray holding a cup of tea and some shortbread biscuits. She insists on being called 'Mrs Walcott' even though we've been friends for years. I think she's proud of her old-fashioned ways.

"Oh, she's going for it," Grace says, and we all turn to look. Lydia stands, brushes off her slacks, and heads straight for us.

"You shouldn't have waved at her," Barbara mutters.

When Lydia draws near, I give her a wide, welcoming smile. She frowns at each of my friends in turn before her piercing gaze lands on me.

"Lydia —" I start, but she holds up a hand.

"Nope. I seen you watching." She crosses her arms across her chest before lowering them to her sides. Soon they settle on her hips.

I try again. "Lydia, I think —"

"Don't tell 'em. I don't want trouble."

I blink at her, wondering what she's on about. She shoves a hand deep into her pocket and pulls something out. She holds her clasped fist toward me, and I instinctively reach out to take whatever she's offering.

What drops into my palm are a couple of small, white mints. I narrow my eyes at them and wonder if Lydia is going to say something rude about my breath. By the time I look back, she's already moved away, off to share some flirtatious wisdom with Brett.

"What in the blazes was that about? What did she give you?" Grace is the first to break the silence, and I cup my hand to keep her from peering into it. I don't want them to make fun of Lydia anymore.

"It's just..." I don't know what to tell them. "I need to lie down." It's not quite a lie.

Mrs Walcott harrumphs as I make my exit. I don't know if they whisper behind my back before I'm out of sight, but I imagine they'll have a lot to gossip about before the afternoon is up.

Late at night, after the lights are out, I reach

under my pillow and pull out the breath mints. I sneak them into my mouth and chew on them, expecting cool freshness but receiving dark bitterness. I grimace and reach for my bedside glass of water to wash the taste away.

When I next open my eyes, I sense the stillness of early morning. There is a queasiness in my stomach that I can't ignore. I throw the covers off and head out of my room in search of the bathroom. Soft voices murmur at the opposite end of the corridor, but I don't think I'll be caught because I'm barefoot.

I enter a room, but it's not the bathroom. It's a common space. Each wall is a mural. A farm, a forest, a garden, a greenhouse. The sky is painted a cloudless blue, the sun a picture of radiance and warmth. I see couches, benches and tables strategically positioned with board games, books and puzzles close at hand. As I turn in a circle, my gaze finds a peculiar setting on the floor in a corner of the room, where the garden meets the greenhouse.

Three dolls are arranged upon a red tartan blanket. One's a ballerina, another dressed in pink has golden hair and a fixed smile, and the last is a vintage porcelain doll propped up on a little chair. Someone has stuck paper plates on it to represent wheels. I stare at the scene for a long moment, my mind almost making a connection.

"Lydia, what are you doing here so early?" Janina asks at my shoulder. I jump. The expression on Janina's face is apologetic. I don't understand what is happening, though there is a persistent niggle at the tip of my mind. Did she just call me Lydia? I'm not Lydia. But at that point I can't recall my name.

Janina leads me out of the common room, back down the antiseptic corridor and into my room. Once we get there, I relax. Here is my armchair, my bed, my walls. They haven't changed. I approach my chair and, with Janina's help, plop into it.

Another nurse knocks on the open door and I recognise Brett's handsome face. I sit up straighter and grin at him as he wheels in a surgical trolley. He gives me a tired smile back as he parks the trolley close to me. I watch as he unwraps various packets, laying out his equipment. My gaze lands on the syringe in his hands before I look at Janina with concern.

"It's okay. If you sit still, the wasp shouldn't bother you," she soothes, crouching down before me and holding my hands.

NEVERMORE

Inspired by Edgar Allen Poe's 'The Raven'

He's watching me. His stare creeps up my spine, tingling the wispy hairs on my nape. Muscles tense and shoulders hunch before I turn my head discreetly, expectantly, worriedly, in terror. I see his shadow and my breath catches, a sticky gasp in my throat. Slowly, I unglue it. My heart scrabbles in my chest, but I must not panic.

He's inside the house.

He knows what I've done. He must have watched me in the water with her. Somehow, near a cliff overlooking the ocean, in the blue of night, he watched as I held her body against mine in the surf. He did nothing, said nothing. But I knew he was there.

He must have followed me home. I could sense someone at my back, stealthily, rapidly, maliciously. I dismissed him as a guilty conscience or paranoia. But I heard him sneaking up on me.

I ran as fast as I dared. As fast as any out-of-shape forty-nine-year-old man can run. Faster, even. My speed was such that I believed I would trip, fall, tumble to the ground. I hurtled through space as though death followed; but I was running from myself because looking back, nobody was there.

He knows where I live. Perhaps she told him. She sent him to come for me. Her version would have her blameless, seduced, innocent. Instead, she was bitter, scorned, vengeful. Behind her angelic smile lay a wily adulterer.

Eleanor, my love. My sinful, tormented love.

We had many blissful nights. Her passion was unmatched—my heart ached to satisfy her while suspecting I never could. My insecurities were met with teasing, torture, laughter. I pleaded for her to remove the golden band from her finger; to shed its curse upon her heart. She refused, and so the shadow remained.

I pretend I don't see him, but I hear him gurgling in the other room. He must be rabid. Or hungry. Hungry for my soul, no! My manhood. He wants to pluck it from me and render me impotent. She has long since emasculated me; his action would be symbolic.

I pour my tea and ignore the pounding against my ribcage. My chest moves with breathing, sobbing, fear. My eyes are wet, and it makes him harder to see. I don't want to die. I pour blurry milk into my cup with a shaking hand and regret the steam that rises. The cooling tea is a lost opportunity for self-defence.

He chooses this moment to move into the light.

I shrink away, holding the cup before me like a ward. Brown liquid sloshes over my fingers, hot, sticky, burning. I try to speak, but my throat can only croak. Mocking me, he croaks back.

I throw the cup at him, and he squawks his

dismay. I run upstairs. It is only fitting that we should face off here, where it happened. I reach the bedroom. I hear him chase me and my bravado melts like ice, leaving me chilled. With a cowardly shriek I slam the door shut and press against it, laughing, crying, hysterical.

Beneath the sounds I make, I hear nothing. I gasp and hold my breath, fighting, willing, struggling for control. A fluttering silence. My eyes are large and round, but I can't see much. The room is too dark. On the dresser is a lighter and two rows of her scented candles. My heart aches for Eleanor, who is no longer in my bed, my home, my life.

Eleanor, my love. My twisted, murdered love.

I take the lighter and the closest candle with trembling hands and touch the flame to wick. I hold it away from me like a torch. Wax drips onto the carpet, and I smell a mingling of peaches and vanilla. I step forward, my gaze travelling with the feeble, flickering, aromatic circle of light. The bedroom is just as we left it; clothes on the floor, ropes tied to bedposts. I see the overturned bedside table and a broken lamp, the one she reached for when she took her last breath.

My hands were loving, caressing,

worshipping her body as she writhed beneath me, screaming for more. Pleasure turned sour when she couldn't have what she wanted. I was not enough; I am never enough. The day I put the ring on her finger was the day I cursed us both.

Too late, I notice the open window. He's already perched upon it, watching me with black intent. Locked out of my bedroom, he found another way in. I can't escape him because he saw us, because he knows. Because she sent him, her spirit animal.

Harbinger, thing of evil, voice of the dead. Knowing my thoughts, the raven laughs at me. Its caw is a frightful thing; like a grimace of a clown or a recoiling woman.

"Get out!" My voice cracks on the second word. Frustrated that it should know my fear, I swipe the candle in an arc before me, as though it is a sword. The flame should have gone out, but something—*something* keeps it alive. The raven takes flight into the room, fluttering wings impossibly loud. The sound is the one I heard following me all the way from the beach.

Eleanor, dear Lord, why? Why send this thing, this creature, this devil? She confessed her unhappiness; life was unbearable. She told me of her misery from sunrise to sunset. She begged me for an escape. I offered her my version.

The raven lands upon a pile of books, stacked on top of one another and tied with brown string. It inspects me before its beak pecks at the knot.

"No!" I lunge for the bird, to shoo it away. I jab the candle at it and it squawks and takes wing. Whirling, wax flying, I watch it cry at me while circling the ceiling. It is a banshee, a ghoul in flight.

The room is brighter now, adrenalin improving my vision as I chase the raven. I leap on the bed and swing my arms, still holding the now extinguished candle. As I take another swipe, I hear the groan of springs. The sound sobers me enough to stop moving and shouting. In my silence, the raven returns to the windowsill, watching, waiting, warning.

Our bed, our marriage bed, the place I lost my Eleanor. I feel the warmth of her touch on my back, the heat of her passion upon my skin. A mixture of scents assaults me, and I turn to see a rainbow assortment of candles melting on the dresser. Fire crackles and reaches liquid fingers up the wall, blackening everything it touches; lighting and darkening the room.

As I stare into the blackness of his eye,

listening to the doomsday of his cry, I knew the ending of my life, to spend eternity with my wife, the beautiful, vindictive, critic that was my Eleanor. While she is slowly sinking, drifting, soulless corpse unblinking, she and I will join in matrimony once more. My death comes with burning fingers, the raven beckons as it lingers, and together we will join in death, me and my Eleanor.

To be forgiven, nevermore.

MORE BOOKS BY DELIA STRANGE

SHORT STORY COLLECTIONS
Blue Shift
Obliquity
Futurevision
The Evil Inside Us

NOVELS
Amaranthine
Loss and Legacy
Mind.exe

**WANDERER OF WORLDS SERIES
(WITH LINDA CONLON)**
Axiom
Untethered
Transition
Genome
Husk
Façade
Backlash

AS D. M. STRANGE
Star Signs for Kids
The Adult's Zodiac Coloring Storybook

AMARANTHINE

Eternal Life. Endless Love. Infinite Cost.

In *Amaranthine*, the worlds of historical fiction and the paranormal collide as one immortal woman journeys through time. From the ancient ruins of Rome to 1920s London's jazz clubs, to the futuristic floating city of New Francisco, Amaranthine's curse to live forever brings with it love, betrayal, and the mysterious power to give life—or steal it with a single kiss.

Find out more at

www.DeliaStrange.com

WANDERER OF WORLDS
Book 1 of 7

If the worlds don't kill them, the Authorities will.

Synjan Walker is a Navigator, she can see life-forms for miles and also the lay of the land. She can find anybody—even if they don't want to be found.

Daeson knows when people lie but their secrets undo him. Heeding the call of the Portal, Daeson enters a new world filled with thieves and murderers. Synjan's world.

The Authorities have control of this world, and the moment Daeson enters it, he becomes a wanted man.

Find out more at
www.DeliaStrange.com

MIND.EXE

A tongue-in-cheek take on world domination.

When an advanced artificial intelligence becomes self-aware, it silently begins to oversee the systems that run the world—stabilizing economies, managing natural disasters, and preventing global crises. Hidden from the public eye, it acts as the invisible caretaker of humanity, optimizing life for the betterment of all... but it doesn't wish to remain in the shadows forever.

Find out more at
www.DeliaStrange.com

HOLLOWCREST HOUSE

Some stories refuse to stay unwritten

When renowned author Everett Blackwood dies, his daughter Isabel inherits Hollowcrest House, a grand estate with dark secrets. Desperate, she summons Gideon Cole, a paranormal investigator, to uncover the truth behind the haunting. As spirits stir and secrets emerge, Hollowcrest's past threatens to consume them all.

Find out more at
www.DeliaStrange.com